# PARAPLUIE

## A Fable

WB ARNAUD

OLD SHRIMP ROAD
PRESS

Key West, Florida

*Book Cover by wb Arnaud*
*(AI-assisted using Microsoft Designer)*

*Illustrations by wb Arnaud*
*(AI-generated using Microsoft Designer)*

ISBN 978-1-971363-01-1 (Paperback)

1st edition 2025

*For my sister*
*—wba*

# Author's Note

*The idea for Parapluie began, as many of my ideas do— in the rain.*

*Years ago, while browsing in a crooked little shop on New Oxford Street in London, I ran across a parrot-headed umbrella—too whimsical to ignore, too alive to be ordinary.*

*Later, in a Paris storm, the thought returned: what if such an umbrella had a life of its own, passing quietly from hand to hand, shaping the lives it sheltered?*

*From that small curiosity came this story: a tale of rain, resilience, and the gentle magic we all carry.*

*Que la pluie vous parle.*

*— wb Arnaud*

"*Great perils have this beauty, that they bring to light the fraternity of strangers.*"

— *Victor Hugo*

## Language Note

You'll find bits of French woven through this tale—
names, street corners, the odd turn of phrase. Whenever
the meaning matters, it is either carried in the sentence
itself or translated close by. At the end of the book,
you'll also find a short *glossaire* should you wish to
linger over any of the words.

Say the words aloud, if you wish. Even imperfectly
spoken, they'll sound like Paris.

# Table des Matières

LE CONTEUR
"The Storyteller"
PROLOGUE

# PROLOGUE

## LE CONTEUR
*The Storyteller*

aris. The City of Light.

Everyone says it—usually with a sigh and a shrug, like they coined it themselves. And a city of light she is: lanterns glow on her bridges, lamps cast halos along the boulevards, and above the cabarets, gaslight flickers like hesitation.

But Paris—ah, Paris… She always finds her puddles. She is as much a city of rain as she is of light. In the storm, she whispers her secrets, cobblestones like black mirrors, gutters running quick with silver, the air sharp with the scent of smoke and rising bread.

You know Paris in the sun. But do you know her in the storm?

Tonight, the storm keeps us here—in this crowded café, windows fogged, the air thick with tobacco and onion soup. Coats drip on their hooks. Outside, streetlamps swim in halos. Strangers are pressed shoulder to shoulder, and by chance, you find yourself beside me—unintended companions for the evening.

Thunder rattles the shutters. Rain drums against the glass. The fire is warm, the wine flows—and as storms do, it loosens old stories from the heart.

The look in your eye says you wonder about the man

who speaks to you now—hair silvered by years, face weathered, voice worn by smoke, yet softened by time.

Think of me only as a companion for this storm. That's enough. The rest will come, as the rain decides.

My name?

Here, they call me *le conteur*—"the storyteller." Storms and wine tend to loosen my tongue. Make of that what you will.

True story? It doesn't matter; perhaps it never happened at all. What matters is the tale—and mine is a magical one.

The tale of an object—small enough to carry, large enough to change a life. Shaped by storm and kindness, it passes from hand to hand, never lingering too long, never lost, only arriving when it's most needed. Some say it brings shelter; others, change. I wouldn't swear to it, mind you. I only know this: wherever it appears, lives shift. The timid find courage. The grieving discover they can still rise. The lonely learn they were never quite alone.

Their stories cling to it still, like raindrops on silk.

So—fill your glass. Draw your chair closer to the fire. Listen.

Let's begin where it all started: in a crooked little shop not far from here—the shop of a man who forged wonders from storms.

LE FORGERON DE LA PLUIE
"The Blacksmith of Rain"
LIVRE I

# LIVRE 1 :
# LE FORGERON DE LA PLUIE

## LA BOUTIQUE TORDUE
*The Crooked Shop*

On Rue des Martyrs, there stood a shop that leaned so heavily into the street, it seemed always on the verge of tumbling into the gutter. Its shutters sagged, its paint peeled, and ivy curled around its windows like green lace. Moss capped the roof tiles. The walls were heavy with centuries of soot and smoke. Yet the little brass bell above the door still rang brightly, and the lamplight inside glowed as warmly as a hearth.

Parisians called it *la boutique tordue*—"the crooked shop"—and they said it had been there longer than anyone remembered. Children whispered that the storms themselves were kept on its shelves, and some grown men muttered a prayer and quickened their step when passing after dark.

Step through the door, and the air changed. It smelled of polish and rain, of oiled wood and damp wool. A faint tang of brass and leather hung in the air, and if one listened closely, there was always the soft patter of raindrops—though whether it came from outside or from the umbrellas themselves was impossible to tell. Racks crowded every corner, where silks stretched in muted blacks and browns, their carved handles plain or ornate, the wood rich with the patina of careful hands and oil. They leaned together like a forest waiting for weather, their canopies brushing against one another with a hushed rustle whenever the door opened.

It was said that the bell above the door chose when to ring, and that rain never puddled at its threshold.

At the heart of it all worked Guillaume De Saint-Aubin, *le Forgeron de la Pluie*—"the Blacksmith of Rain." Some called him a craftsman, others a legend. He was a man of steady hands and patient silence, known throughout Montmartre for umbrellas that never faltered. When Paris's storms turned others inside out, Guillaume's creations held their shape such that the rain itself paused to admire his work.

Guillaume was not a young man, though not so old as to be stooped. His hair had gone silver at the temples, his back bore the faint bend of years spent at the bench, and his eyes carried the softness of one who saw storms as companions rather than enemies. His fingers were nicked from blades, rough with callus, stained faintly with oil and dye. He lived alone, though not unhappily; the neighborhood pigeons occasionally dropped by uninvited for counsel. His company was wood shavings that curled like ribbons across the floor, silk bolts stacked like precious cloth in a dressmaker's shop, brass ribs that clinked like coins in their jars, and the rhythm of rain on the windowpane.

Outside, Paris steamed. Rain washed the cobblestones to a black shine, and horses splashed through the gutters, their breath rising in clouds. Gas lamps hissed and blurred to halos in the mist. The air tasted of wet stone, coal smoke, and roasted chestnuts from a vendor braving the storm beneath an awning. A drunk sang a wavering *chanson* beneath a dripping archway, while cats darted across the street, their fur slick to their bones. Even the rain fell crookedly along Rue des Martyrs.

Inside, the shop was the eye of the storm, warm and timeless. Guillaume stitched, riveted, burnished, the soft hiss of silk following each pull of the needle. His life was measured in seams and sighs, in how customers shook themselves dry on his threshold, in the hush that fell whenever the sky darkened. He loved the storms of Paris, though he never said so aloud. They gave him purpose. They gave him song.

It was on such a night, when thunder rolled above the rooftops, the gutters gushed like rivers, and lightning painted the streets green, that the bell above the door jangled, and a stranger crossed the crooked shop's threshold. The bell's chime wavered once and died, its echo lingering in the rafters, mingling with the scent of rain and brass. Guillaume looked up from his bench, needle paused mid-stitch, as the storm drew a breath and held it.

# L'ÉTRANGER
*The Stranger*

A figure stood framed in the crooked doorway, silhouetted for an instant by lightning that bleached the street bone-white. No rain clung to his coat. His boots bore no trace of mud. Not a single drop marked his hat.

Guillaume's hand, still holding the threaded needle, froze. The shop itself froze, shadows pressing closer, rows of umbrellas leaning toward the stranger in wordless respect.

The storm outside clattered and hissed, but within the crooked shop, a quiet settled—heavy, deliberate. Even the brass ribs in their jars ceased their faint tinkling. The patter that had always whispered among the racks was gone. The lamplight faltered, then flared.

The stranger was neither young nor old, his face weathered like driftwood—smooth in places, deeply grooved in others. The lines could have been carved by laughter or grief; it was impossible to tell which. His mouth carried the suggestion of a smile, though not the kind that comforts—it was the smile of someone who knows endings as well as beginnings. His eyes stayed hidden beneath the brim of his hat.

Guillaume's heart beat faster.

The man's gloved hand emerged from his coat and drew forth a small bundle wrapped in cloth so dark that it drank the lamplight. With deliberate care, he set it on Guillaume's bench. The bundle gave a muted sigh as it

met the wood—barely a whisper, yet it filled the shop
like thunder.

# UN CADEAU
*A Gift*

Guillaume's hand hovered above the bundle, his breath shallow, the storm's glow flickering across the black cloth. The fabric absorbed all light, its folds deep as night. Its edges hummed faintly in his imagination like a taut string. For a long moment, he dared not touch it.

The stranger did not move, did not speak; his presence pinned the air in place, heavy with expectation. Even the clock on the wall, usually diligent in its ticking, lost the courage to mark the seconds.

At last, Guillaume's fingers closed on the cloth. It was cool beneath his skin and faintly damp, like stone warmed by rain. He drew it back with slow care.

Within lay a handle, carved from wood—but not like any he knew. Its grain shimmered with colors that shifted between green and gold, with mossy forest and sunlit fields flowing through its veins. It was shaped into the head of a parrot—proud beak curved and dignified, eyes set with stones that caught the lamplight and fractured it into tiny shards, glowing with some hidden fire that stirred behind them.

The craft was beyond masterful. Each feather, etched in astonishing detail, seemed ready to lift at a whisper of wind. The curve of the neck carried a natural grace, as though the bird might lean forward and speak. The polish of the beak reflected more than light; it hinted at thought, at vigilance. Guillaume felt the hairs rise on his arms. This was no ornament, no curiosity from an exotic market. This was a work that bore intention, carved with more than mere tools.

Outside, the tempest pressed against the windows, lightning flashing like struck flint, freezing the parrot's head in stark brilliance. In those flashes, the eyes burned—first emerald, then amber, then a pale, eerie blue. Shadows stretched long and curious across the bench, and the umbrellas in their racks rustled faintly, though no draft stirred them.

Guillaume's hands—hands that had shaped a thousand canopies, stitched a million seams—now trembled like an apprentice's as he lifted the piece. Its weight was at once slight and immense—the storm, compressed into wood.

He opened his mouth to speak, but no words came. The stranger inclined his head slightly, granting permission. Guillaume pressed the parrot's head to his chest for a heartbeat, feeling the thrum of his own heart answer it like a drum. And in that rhythm, something awakened— not in the wood, but in himself.

Beyond the windows, the storm rumbled low, and Paris sighed.

# LES RÈGLES
*The Rules*

uillaume stood with the carved handle in his hands, its feathers catching the lamplight as though each line held its own flame. The weight of it unsettled him—not heavy, but solemn, the way a crown must feel when first set upon a brow. He did not speak; neither did the stranger. The crooked shop listened, still and intent.

At last, the stranger moved and fixed Guillaume with eyes that were not easily met, rain and sunlight both having taken root within them. When he finally spoke, his voice was measured, low, resonant—the echo of a cathedral nave.

*"Pas à vendre."*

Not to be sold.

The words fell like stones dropped into a well. The lamp flickered, and Guillaume felt the phrase sink into him.

*"Pas à garder."*

Not to be kept.

The syllables tolled like a distant bell, final and inarguable. The umbrellas in their racks rustled faintly.

*"Pour un cœur vrai."*

For a true heart.

The words were spoken with quiet force, dread and joy entwined. Guillaume's hands trembled; he tightened his grip to calm himself.

The shop had grown hushed and expectant. The shadows stretched, the lamp faltered, and the wind leaned against the shutters.

The stranger, deliberate, calm, and with a nod, turned toward the door.

Something inside Guillaume gave way. His throat rasped as he tried to shape the questions pressing against his chest. "But … these rules," he whispered, the words rough, broken. "Why must it be bound so? Not sold, not kept … true heart? What do they mean?"

He lifted his eyes from the carved handle, questions spilling into the dim air—only to find the doorway already empty. The bell above the crooked shop gave a hollow ring as the stranger stepped back out into the storm.

A peal of thunder cracked overhead, and the lamp guttered and died, plunging the shop into darkness.

For a full minute, the world held its breath—only the hammering of the rain, only the memory of those three rules. Then, slowly, the light returned, the flame trembling back to life.

Guillaume sat very still, the object heavy in his hands, the rules echoing in the silence.

# LA FORGE

*The Forge*

When the lamp's flame steadied once more, Guillaume remained frozen at his bench, the carved handle heavy in his hands. The storm pressed close to the shutters, growling like a beast deciding whether to pounce or withdraw.

The clock resumed its ticking, hesitant. The rules still rang in his ears:

*"Pas à vendre"*—not to be sold.

*"Pas à garder"*—not to be kept.

*"Pour un cœur vrai"*—for a true heart.

They were like iron bars struck against stone, resonant and inescapable. Guillaume did not understand them, yet their weight pressed into him as surely as the carved handle pressed against his palm.

Slowly, with the reverence of a priest lifting a relic, he set the piece upon his bench. His fingers moved without thought, reaching for the familiar tools of his craft: brass ribs, lacquered shafts, silk dyed the color of midnight. Around him, the crooked shop exhaled, wood and shadow shifting as though aware of what was to come.

He measured, cut, stitched, the needle whispering through silk, the ribs clicking into place with the finality of bones locking in their joints. His hands, roughened by decades of labor, worked with a precision beyond his own. Outside, the thunder softened, the rain slowing to a rhythm that matched his stitching.

As the hours passed, the shop filled with the scent of oil and dye, of heated metal and polished wood. Exhaustion settled into his shoulders, but he did not stop. Each seam, each rivet, each fold of silk was part of a ritual destined for him. The handle, when at last he set it into place, sighed against the frame, as though it had been waiting for this union.

Outside, the storm gathered itself one last time. A bolt tore through the sky, thunder rolling so deep that it trembled in Guillaume's chest. The lamplight shuddered. Then—silence, save for the soft hiss of rain.

A scent rose in the quiet: iron and roses, sharp and sweet.

When dawn crept pale over Montmartre, Guillaume leaned back. Before him lay an umbrella unlike any he had ever made—a canopy of deep midnight silk, ribs like wet gold, and at its base, the parrot's head, watchful and alive with silent fire.

Guillaume bowed his head, weary, awed, and afraid.

He whispered into the silence: *"L'ouvrage."*

The work. The masterpiece.

# LE GARDIEN
*The Keeper*


For three weeks, Guillaume kept *l'ouvrage* close, unable to part with it. The rules rang in his ears—*"Pas à vendre. Pas à garder. Pour un cœur vrai."*—yet still he hesitated. Each day, he told himself he would pass it on tomorrow. Always tomorrow.

Customers came into the crooked shop, their eyes drawn to it at once. Some offered money—good money, more than he might earn in a season. Others begged, enchanted by its gleam. Guillaume always refused, his hand tightening on the object before he quickly set it out of sight. He was not proud of himself—of the sharpness in his voice, nor of the longing that gnawed at him.

On the third evening of the third week, after days of sullen skies, the storm finally broke, and Montmartre sparkled with sunshine. Guillaume, restless, took *l'ouvrage* and went for a walk. He had not strolled the quarter at night in many years, but tonight he was lighter, younger.

For no reason he could name, he flicked it open, and beneath its midnight canopy, the world glowed brighter, the scents of roasting chestnuts, tobacco smoke, and damp stone sharp in his lungs. Music spilled from taverns, laughter from cafés. People nodded as he passed; one woman smiled at him like they were old friends.

He could not explain it, but he was alive—truly alive. Paris had welcomed him back.

He lingered at a crowded cabaret near Place Pigalle, sipping a glass of wine, letting the hum of voices and the scrape of violins warm him more than the drink. The night was charmed, every sound and face touched by some private glow.

Outside, a thin figure pressed against the fogged glass, eyes wide, lips parted, drinking in the music itself. The boy, perhaps eight years old, wore ragged clothes that hung loose on his frame, his gaze never wavering from the bow moving across the strings. When the tune ended and the room erupted in laughter and clatter, he flinched back into the shadows. From the darkness, his eyes caught on the gleam of midnight silk and a parrot's eerie gaze—and held.

When at last Guillaume stepped into the street, *l'ouvrage* was balanced lightly in his hand. The air was cool, rinsed clean by the storm, and he drew it deep into his lungs. Paris sparkled beneath her veil of rain—lamplight pooling in the gutters, rooftops glistening, every breath carrying the mingled scents of smoke, bread, and wet stone.

The city breathed with him, her heartbeat in time with his own. For the first time in his life, he was weightless.

Then—a blur.

The ragged boy burst from the darkness, clothes flapping like torn sails—eyes fixed not on Guillaume, but on the gleaming shaft he held. Small, quick hands snatched at *l'ouvrage*. Guillaume staggered back, startled, his fingers tightening instinctively. For an instant, they grappled in silence, his roughened hands against the boy's wiry grip. The child's eyes flashed up at him—wide, wild, desperate.

Guillaume gasped—as though he had grasped not a

boy's wrist, but a living spark.

The thief wrenched hard, twisting his body with the feral strength of hunger, and *l'ouvrage* tore free. Guillaume lurched forward with a cry, nearly falling into the gutter as the boy bolted into the street, the dark shaft clutched tight against his chest. Gaslight splashed across the scene, and voices rose at once: a woman shrieked, a drunkard laughed, someone shouted, "Stop him!" Hands reached from the crowd, but the boy slipped between them, ephemeral as smoke, his small frame vanishing and reappearing among startled revelers. Chairs overturned, wine spilled, and curses rang out as the chase swept into the heart of Pigalle.

Guillaume pushed harder, fear and desperation tightening around his ribs—not for his craft, not for his pride, but for something he knew was larger than himself. He plunged after the boy into the tangle of streets. The lane reeked of wet cobblestones, horse sweat, and spilled wine. Laughter and curses tangled in the air as passersby shouted, some cheering the chase, others jeering.

A cart rolled across the way, and Guillaume nearly collided with its wheels, stumbling but pressing on. The boy darted between legs and barrels, his ragged form flashing in and out of lantern light. Guillaume's lungs burned, his boots slapping the wet cobblestones. The streets narrowed around him, echoing with shouts and the pounding of his boots. Rain streamed from the eaves, silver in the lamplight.

*Pas à vendre.*

Not to be sold.

The boy's thin frame darted through the glow and

shadow, bare feet splashing through the gutters, clutching the umbrella.

*Pas à garder.*

Not to be kept.

Guillaume's breath came ragged. He saw the curve of the boy's shoulders, the hunger in his movement, the wild need to survive. It was not theft—it was longing, hunger.

It was the same rain falling on them both.

*Pour un cœur vrai.*

For a true heart.

Guillaume slowed. The thought came sudden and sharp, rising above the din of the chase: *Let it go.*

He faltered, chest heaving, the will to give overtaking the need to hold.

A weight lifted, quiet and certain.

*L'ouvrage* had chosen its new *gardien.*

In that instant, the shadows ahead shifted.

A heavy figure stepped from the darkness— broad-shouldered and red-faced, dark captain's coat cut longer than the other policemen's, its oversized brass buttons clunky and ornate. A cigarette hung from his teeth, its ember glowing each time he drew breath, casting brief flashes of red across his wet face. A short *bâton* swung from his belt, tapping against his thigh as he walked. His eyes were small and sharp beneath the brim of his cap—eyes that measured how much a man could take before he broke.

The *rousse* wrenched *l'ouvrage* from the boy's grasp with a snarl and swung it back at him, hitting him squarely in the forehead. The parrot's beak met bone—a single, sickening crack that silenced the street. The child fell, blood bright against the stones, then vanished, crawling into the dark like a wounded animal.

Guillaume's mouth opened, but no sound came. A rat scuttled through the puddle between them, streaking the water red as it passed. The officer pressed *l'ouvrage* back into Guillaume's trembling hands. The shaft was as cold as ice.

"Watch your things," he muttered, before striding off into the night.

Guillaume stared after the boy's shadow, guilt gnawing at his chest. He turned toward home.

Across the square, a silhouette stood beneath a flickering lamp, coat dark, face hidden. Then the wind shifted, and there was nothing but rainwater glimmering on the stones.

Back at the crooked shop, the lamps felt dimmer, the walls closer. Guillaume set *l'ouvrage* on the bench and sat beside it, listening to the stormless silence of the night. The joy of the evening had drained away, leaving only weariness and dread. He thought of the boy's cry, the cruel hand that had struck him, and how the will to let go had come only a heartbeat too late.

Sleep would not come. Each time he closed his eyes, he saw the boy's thin figure running, the shaft clutched desperately against his chest. He saw the police captain with the strange buttons. He heard the crack of the blow again and again. He pressed his palms to his ears, but the sound would not leave him.

By dawn, Guillaume had given up on sleep. He sat watching the faint light creep across the floorboards, *l'ou-*

*vrage* motionless beside him. Whatever power it carried, it was no longer his to command.

Outside, the wind began to rise again.

LE COMMIS TIMIDE
"The Timid Clerk"
LIVRE II

# LIVRE II :
# LE COMMIS TIMIDE

## SANS NOM
*Without a Name*

The morning after his restless night, Guillaume rose with heavy limbs. The shop felt close, its shadows uneasy, and even the familiar scent of varnish and silk could not soothe him. An errand waited—dull, necessary, one of those bureaucratic rituals that keep a tradesman tethered to the city. The ledger of licenses was due, and if he failed to sign it, the penalties would be steep. With a sigh, he gathered his papers—and without quite knowing why, he took *l'ouvrage* as well. It weighed upon him, demanding to be present.

The Hôtel de Ville office was a cavern of stone and dust, its high ceiling dripping with shadows. Clerks sat behind wooden counters in obedient rows, pens scratching endlessly, eyes dulled by repetition. The air hung thick with the scent of ink and damp wool, and beneath it lingered the slow decay of paper and time. Lines shuffled forward; boots tapped; someone coughed in the echoing gloom. Guillaume took his place in the queue, papers tucked beneath his arm, *l'ouvrage* resting by his boot.

When at last his turn arrived, he stepped up to a desk where a young clerk hunched over his forms. The man was slight, his jacket too narrow across the shoulders, the cuffs frayed, the elbows polished smooth by years of work. Ink stains marked his fingers and the edge of his jaw, where he must have rubbed at an absent thought. His hair, dark and overgrown, clung to his temples. In this hall of stone and mildew, he was *sans nom*—nameless, just another clerk blurred among the rows.

He avoided meeting Guillaume's eyes, speaking instead to the papers before him. The desk was his refuge: pens aligned in perfect rows, inkwell precisely centered, each stack of forms squared to the edge, as if order itself might shield him from the chaos of voices around him. Before touching any object, he brushed a fingertip across it—a quiet ritual of reassurance.

"Name," he murmured at last, dipping his pen.

"Guillaume De Saint-Aubin," came the reply, rough with fatigue.

The clerk wrote it down, blotting the ink with care. He asked for trade, address, license number—all in a voice scarcely above a whisper. Guillaume answered, laying each document in turn upon the desk. At last, without thinking, he rested *l'ouvrage* beside them.

The clerk's hand faltered. A moment before, his eyes had been dull; now they fixed on the object. The carved handle caught the meager light—impossibly bright in that dim hall—and the young man drew in a sharp breath. His fingers hovered, unwilling to touch, yet unable to turn away. In that instant, it happened—a shift, a stirring.

*Pas à vendre. Pas à garder. Pour un cœur vrai.*

Guillaume studied the clerk: the tremor in his lips, the hunger in his gaze that was not greed, but something more fragile—a yearning for courage, for color, for a

spark in the gray drudgery of ink and paper.

Guillaume's chest tightened. And he knew.

Not for the boy who had stolen it—though the boy had been chosen by it. Not for the officer who had wielded it like a weapon. But here, in this gray hall where men were ground into numbers, where dignity came only from order and ink—here was a heart that yearned not for power, but for something much simpler: To be seen. To matter. To stand upright in a world that bent him low.

"Sign here," the clerk whispered, though his eyes never left *l'ouvrage*.

Guillaume dipped the pen and wrote his name with deliberate strokes. Beneath it, as if it were nothing more than a tradesman's flourish, he inscribed:

*Pas à vendre.*

*Pas à garder.*

*Pour un cœur vrai.*

The clerk frowned faintly, lips moving as he read. He looked up at last, startled and confused, mouth half open to speak—but Guillaume was already gathering his papers, leaving *l'ouvrage* on the desk.

Given freely at last.

The bell of the great hall tolled the hour. In the stale light of the office, the timid clerk sat frozen, the umbrella before him like a midnight sky folded into his hands, the strange words inked into the city's record binding him quietly to its mystery.

The scent of iron and roses filled the air.

# LE PREMIER JOUR
*The First Day*

The clerk did not move for some time after Guillaume left. The great hall's voices swelled and fell around him—the stamping of papers, the hiss of pens, the scrape of boots—but he sat motionless with *l'ouvrage* before him. Its midnight canopy was folded tight, the carved handle watching him with a patient eye. He scarcely breathed, afraid the object might vanish like a dream at dawn.

"Next!" barked one of his colleagues, jolting him back to the world.

For a moment, he thought the hall itself had grown quieter, that even the scratching pens had slowed. He blinked, uncertain—and the spell broke.

For the remainder of the morning, he kept *l'ouvrage* tucked beneath his desk, but its presence throbbed there like a hidden flame. Each time his colleagues jeered, each time a petitioner was dismissed harshly by another clerk, its weight urged him to stand taller. Once, when a wealthy merchant snapped his fingers impatiently at him, the young man found his voice rising clear and firm: "You will wait your turn, *monsieur*." The words startled even him, yet they hung in the air with undeniable authority. His colleagues exchanged smirks, but the merchant obeyed, muttering under his breath.

They had often mocked him before—his quiet ways, his ink-stained cuffs, the tremor in his voice—but today their laughter slid past him. One called him a poet;

another asked if he would sing lullabies to the petitioners next. Yet the sting was duller now, their words broken against an unseen shield.

The hall also changed in small ways. The ink seemed darker, the parchment cleaner, the air less stifled. When he handed documents back, petitioners met his gaze with something closer to gratitude than frustration. A quiet warmth gathered in his chest each time.

At noon, when the clerks drifted away for their meal, he lingered. He drew *l'ouvrage* from beneath the desk and held it in both hands. The wood was warm, even in the cold room. Slowly, reverently, he opened the canopy. Light from the high windows caught the silk—deep, lustrous.

For a heartbeat, the cavernous hall was transformed—the mildew faded, the dust stilled, the shadows softened. He stood not in a dreary office, but in a quiet glade after rain, the world rinsed clean.

He whispered, *"Magnifique,"* his voice trembling. He closed the canopy and laid *l'ouvrage* carefully across his knees. It was no longer only a gift, nor even a mystery. It was a calling. A responsibility.

That evening, as he left the Hôtel de Ville, the old weight returned. The narrow streets beckoned—his usual route, head down, unseen. Yet tonight his hand rested on *l'ouvrage*, and something made him take the wider boulevard instead. A drizzle had begun. He hesitated, then unfurled the canopy. Beneath its shelter, he stood taller, the rain itself bowing aside.

Passersby glanced at him—not mockingly, but with curiosity, even respect. One child tugged at her mother's sleeve, pointing at the parrot's head. The clerk, timid no more in that moment, tipped *l'ouvrage* slightly toward her in greeting. The girl grinned, her eyes wide with delight.

He did not go straight home. He wandered through streets he had long avoided, where cafés spilled golden light and laughter across the cobblestones. Once, he would have hurried past with eyes downcast, but tonight he lingered at the door. Through the fogged glass, strangers laughed over wine and cheese.

His shoulders tensed. *I should walk on.* He always had before.

The waiter glanced up, met his eyes, and smiled. "A table, *monsieur?* The terrace is nearly full, but we can make room."

The old voice inside whispered to refuse, to hurry home. But the clerk's mouth said, *"Merci,"* and to his astonishment, he stepped inside.

He sat at a small table by the window, sipping coffee slowly, watching the rain trace silver threads down the glass. For the first time in years, he was not invisible.

Later, in a bookshop lit by gas lamps, he found himself drawn to a slim volume of poetry. He touched its spine, hesitated, and then purchased it without apology, carrying it under his arm with quiet pride. The shopkeeper, usually brusque, softened as she handed it over, her eyes flicking once to the midnight canopy.

By the time he reached his small room under the eaves, his chest was alight with something he had never known before—the taste of dignity, of being seen.

He set *l'ouvrage* carefully by his bedside, the book beside it, and whispered into the quiet, *"Merci."*

Outside, the rain whispered against the panes, soft as words half remembered:

*Pas à vendre. Pas à garder. Pour un cœur vrai.*

# LES JOURS SUIVANTS
*The Days After*

The days that followed gathered light around the timid clerk, though he scarcely understood how. Each morning as he walked to the Hôtel de Ville with *l'ouvrage* at his side, the city altered subtly around him—the cobblestones brighter, the river air cleaner, strangers' faces less indifferent. He found himself lifting his head more often, greeting bakers and sweepers with nods he would once have hidden. Some nodded back; a few even smiled. Somewhere beyond the rooftops, the bells of Paris rang.

Inside the hall, the change was quieter, but no less real. Petitioners began to seek his line deliberately, passing by the sharper clerks to stand before his desk. He did not alter his ways—he still spoke gently, still guided trembling hands with patience—but now his voice carried farther, his gestures rippling outward.

The jeers of his colleagues continued, yet their mockery grew thinner, less certain. Once, when the heavyset clerk mocked him openly, a petitioner muttered, "He mocks the only man here who does any actual work." The words struck like a slap.

Before long, his superiors began to take notice. A senior clerk paused at his desk one morning, scanning the neat stacks of papers and the quiet line that moved efficiently before him. *"Travail soigné,"* the man said, almost begrudgingly. Another nodded in passing later that week, remarking that the young man from the back desks seemed to bring order wherever he sat. The words were few, but they settled in his chest like hot coals, smoldering.

Weeks passed, and in the evenings, he ventured beyond his old routine. The café where he had once sat in trembling hesitation now became a place of comfort. Waiters greeted him—not warmly, perhaps, but with recognition. He read his book of poetry there, sipping coffee, listening to the murmur of other lives. Sometimes, when rain pattered against the windows, he opened l'ouvrage just enough to feel its midnight canopy expand.

One evening, a young woman paused to admire it, asking where he'd found such a thing. He smiled—as one who knows the worth of what he holds—and said only, "It found me."

Neighbors who had passed him wordlessly for years now nodded, even exchanged greetings. One child who had watched him the first evening waved whenever she saw him, tugging her mother's hand to stop and stare at the umbrella's gleam. The parrot smiled back. A warmth spread through him each time—not vanity, but the simple balm of being known.

It had been during one of those walks that he discovered the truth of it. A drizzle had begun, light at first, then thickening into a downpour. He unfurled the canopy, expecting the familiar drumming of rain overhead. Yet beneath it, there was only stillness. No drops struck the silk. No wind touched his face. He stopped beneath a lamp and looked down—his shoes were dry, and the cobblestones around him, for a full arm's length in every direction, were dry as well. Beyond that invisible ring, the street glistened and hissed with rain. Within it, silence.

Even his breath was warmer there.

He walked on slowly, testing the edges of the miracle, stepping deliberately into the rain and back. He stood in that circle of calm while the world wept around him. He did not flinch from its wonder.

Yet with each passing day, the weight of Guillaume's strange inscription pressed harder against his heart.

*Pas à vendre.*

*Pas à garder.*

*Pour un cœur vrai.*

The words lingered in his mind like a refrain. He did not know what they asked of him—only that they carried the gravity of a vow. And though his days grew brighter, he intuitively understood that this gift was not meant to remain his forever.

# SOUS LA MÊME PLUIE

*Under the same Rain*

One damp evening, as the clerk walked home, the streets shimmered with lamplight on wet stones. The clerk walked taller now, his step more certain, the book of poetry tucked under his arm.

It was in a narrow lane near Les Halles that he saw the boy. The passage had grown tight, slick with rain. As he turned the corner, a child burst from between two stalls—barefoot, a ragged strip of cloth bound across a scarred brow, a flash of bone and motion—and nearly collided with him. A crust of bread flew from the boy's hand and skittered across the stones. For an instant, they both froze. Something in the boy's eyes—wide, wary, defiant—struck him deeply, as though he were staring at a shadow … or a ghost.

The boy bolted, vanishing into the rain. For a moment, the clerk stood still, heart quickened, the echo of that look burning in his chest. Then, without quite knowing why, he followed.

Ahead, the boy had stopped before a narrow stall wedged under the arcade—a jumble of ribbons, trinkets, and half-broken clocks spread on a damp counter. A heavy man in a stained waistcoat leaned beneath the awning, his smile thin and his tone sharp.

*"Où tu crois aller, gamin? T'as pas fini ton travail"*—"Where do you think you're going, boy? You haven't finished your work."

The faded, uneven lettering on the sign above the

stall read:

## MARCHAND & FILS—
## CURIOSITES ET FILS DE RIEN

The clerk had seen the name before—printed on receipts, muttered by vendors who rolled their eyes after saying it.

The man's voice rose again, cutting through the rain. He struck the broom hard against the cobbles, sending up a spray of dirty water. The boy flinched, shoulders drawn tight, clutching the crust of bread like a shield.

Without quite knowing why, the clerk stepped forward. *"Ça suffit,"* he said, his voice steadier than he expected. The words cut through the rain like a bell.

Le marchand turned, mustache twitching, eyes small and calculating. *"Pardon?"* he said, his smile gone.

The clerk didn't flinch. *"Il n'est qu'un enfant,"* he said firmly—"He is but a child."

*Le marchand* sneered, the mock geniality gone altogether. *"Mêle-toi de tes affaires, monsieur"*—"Mind your own business, sir."

With a muttered curse, he tossed the broom aside and ducked back under his awning, where the light caught the glint of watered wine in a bottle.

For a moment, neither the clerk nor the boy moved. The rain fell between them, soft and unbroken. Then the boy turned and vanished into the crowd.

The city sighed, and the clerk resumed his walk. Lanterns shone with patient light, the rain thinned, and each step fell with the calm certainty of someone no longer lost.

He noticed a violinist playing beneath a café awning, his notes trembling through the rain, and paused to listen, his heart swelling with a quiet kinship. He dropped a coin into the musician's cap—a small gesture, but one he would never have dared before.

When at last he reached his narrow street, he found neighbors gathered in a doorway to escape the weather. The alcove was small and already crowded; shoulders pressed close, coats dark with water, a few unlucky ones still half exposed to the storm. He might have walked past as he always did, but tonight he slowed, lifting *l'ouvrage* above them as he stepped near.

For a moment, the storm forgot itself. Where the doorway had been crowded and dripping, space opened. Those at the edges drew back from the rain with startled laughter, brushing at coats that were suddenly—impossibly—dry. A woman lifted her hands to her hair, finding it smooth and untouched by water. Even the puddles at their feet faded to dull gray stone, while just beyond the threshold, the rain still fell, hard and shining. Within that circle of warmth, soft laughter, and astonished whispers arose the faint scent of iron and roses.

The clerk lingered with them while the storm spent itself. They spoke softly at first, then with ease—neighbors exchanging names, small jokes, even a bit of gossip over the sound of distant thunder. When the rain at last faded to mist, no one hurried inside. They looked at him differently, as though seeing not just the timid clerk, but a man, a neighbor, a friend.

Back in his small room, he placed *l'ouvrage* carefully by the window, where moonlight caught its silk.

Sleep would not come. He lay in the dark, restless,

his pulse too quick. Something unfinished. Something waiting. He didn't know what, only that it pulled at him like a hand on his sleeve, gentle but insistent. He tried to ignore it—turned to the wall, counted his breaths—but the feeling grew stronger, more urgent.

At last, the clerk rose, pulled on his coat, and let his steps carry him once more through the damp streets to the Hôtel de Ville.

# LE REGISTRE OUBLIÉ

*The Forgotten Ledger*

The Hôtel de Ville was dark at that hour, its corridors emptied of voices, its lamps guttering low. The clerk should not have been there, yet his feet had carried him back through the wet streets as though summoned. He slipped inside with the quiet of a trespasser. The night porter, long used to his shy nods, waved him through. And so, he found his familiar desk waiting, ledger spread open like an old companion.

He unstoppered his inkwell, the nib scratching faintly as he drew the first careful line. It was not duty that held him there, nor habit, but something new—a stirring that made him reach for the columns and margins to steady his heart.

On a nearby side table lay a heap of cast-off scraps, margins torn from ledgers too worn for use. He gathered them absently, intending to consign them to the fire.

One page caught him. The hand was careful, cramped, the letters tentative, obviously written by someone trying not to take up space. A single given name had been set down, and beneath it the institutional cadence he knew too well:

*Orphelin, sans demeure.*

He thought of the boy in the square—brow bound with cloth, eyes watchful and wary.

He looked again at the strokes. He knew the hand at once—the shy slope of the *J*, the crowded *u*, the small hesitation before the *n*. His own, younger.

He did not burn the scrap. Instead, he opened his official register, neat with lines of figures, and created an entry—against every rule, against the code that had bound him for years. He wrote the name carefully until the letters stood plain:

### *Julien.*

He sat back, the nib trembling. The ink bled slowly into the paper, fixing what had once been a memory. He knew what it meant—what it would mean if anyone found it. A name written in the city's register was no small thing. It made the nameless real.

But even so, it was not enough. Julien, alone, was still a ledger's orphan—a child without past or place, as easily erased as written.

Henri stared at the word. A name, he thought, must belong to something larger: a family, a sky, a hope.

For a long moment, his pen hovered, unwilling to lift. Then, as though compelled by the page itself, he added a second word—not from duty, nor from any register, but from the sky above the city:

***Pluvier***—"Rainbird."

Closing the book, he placed *l'ouvrage* upon it. The umbrella shifted, silk stirring faintly, as though a breath of warm air had passed through the room. The scent of iron and roses followed.

And the clerk whispered, half aloud, the words that had been entrusted to him: *"Pas à vendre. Pas à garder. Pour un cœur vrai."*

Outside, rain traced its slow rhythm on the stone. Paris listened.

The waiter passes, refills my glass without asking—he knows how these nights go. You shift in your chair, drawing closer to the fire. Outside, the rain owns the night.

You're smiling—I can tell Henri's story pleased you.

Good. That warmth will serve you for what comes next.

LA VEUVE
"The Widow"
LIVRE III

# LIVRE III : LA VEUVE

## LES PAPIERS LIÉS
*Ribbon-Tied Papers*

The morning light fell pale through the tall windows of the Hôtel de Ville, washing the hall in a gray that seeped into each ledger and sigh. Ink and mildew mingled with the smell of damp wool, and boots scraped the stone in a rhythm as weary as the clerks bent over their counters. The hall's voices rose and fell in a monotone tide—petitions, refusals, stamps, dismissals.

At his desk in the row, the timid clerk had arranged his papers neatly, his pens lined up in their narrow tray. Beside his chair, *l'ouvrage* leaned discreetly against the wall, its parrot-headed handle hidden in shadow. He drew strength from it in ways he did not speak of—though whether it was the umbrella itself or something in him that it awakened, he could not say.

It was midmorning when *la veuve*—the widow—appeared.

Her veil was black, drawn low, so that only the pale edge of her chin was visible. Her gloves were still wet from the street, and she moved with the careful grace of someone who had learned to take up as little room as possible. Her hands trembled around her *les papiers liés*—ribbon-tied papers—which she held as though the frayed knot were the last thing tethering her to dignity.

She lowered herself into the chair before a tall clerk with a beaked nose. He did not greet her, did not even look at her. He dragged the bundle toward him and thumbed through the papers with sharp motions, his lips pursed in disdain.

"Incomplete," he said, voice cold as stone.

The rustle of parchment was louder than necessary, meant to shame her.

"Incomplete. Errors. Omissions. I will not waste my time on this."

Her voice fluttered. "Please… I do not understand which forms are… I have written to the archives. I was told—"

He snapped the pages back at her as though they burned him. His chair creaked as he leaned forward, nose sharp in the light.

"*C'est assez!*" he barked, the words cracking across the cavernous hall. "Take it elsewhere. You will not waste my time with your incompetence. Next!"

The entire hall paused at the cruelty of it, the scratching of pens and shuffling of boots faltering for a breath. The widow flinched beneath her veil, clutching the ribbon-tied packet until her hands shook. Tears welled, slipping free as she half rose from the chair, caught between flight and collapse.

The timid clerk had had enough.

His chair scraped back, echoing like a blade drawn from its sheath. Something urged him forward—whether the weight of *l'ouvrage* by his desk or the injustice ringing through the stone, he did not know. He crossed the hall, boots striking hard against the flagstones.

The room turned to watch.

He came to stand beside her, placing himself between them. His eyes locked on his colleague with a glare sharp enough to still the man's tongue.

"That will be all, *monsieur*," he said, his voice low, but edged with iron. "She will be seen properly."

The other clerks shifted uneasily; smirks faded, mutters stilled.

Then he bent toward her, softening. "Madame," he said gently, "please—rest a moment. I will see to it."

He reached for the bundle still clutched in her trembling hands. For an instant, she resisted, then let them go, her fingers loosening as though surrendering a burden. With his free hand, he gestured toward the far desk, and together they crossed the hall, his stride calm, hers faltering, but steadied by his presence.

At his desk, he set the papers down with care, not as scraps of bureaucracy, but the record of a life. She lowered herself into the chair opposite, veil shifting as she drew a long, uneven breath.

"I am Éloïse Aubert. My husband, Luc, was a teacher and a musician," she said at last. "I taught at the École Communale on Rue des Martyrs, but I have not worked since his passing. Without him, the classroom feels empty, and I…" Her voice wavered, catching on silence. She pressed her gloved hands together, as though to keep them from shaking.

Éloïse raised her veil, revealing a face both young and worn, her mouth pale with exhaustion. She steadied her voice as best she could. "I have come to settle his affairs."

Her words trailed into quiet, her eyes lowered to the worn ribbon binding her papers. The hush around them deepened; even the stone walls listened.

The timid clerk looked her fully in the face. He saw the hollows grief had carved beneath her eyes, the weary grace with which she held herself even in humiliation. Something within him settled, like a hand closing around his heart.

"My name is Henri Fournier," he said. "We will take it step by step. No rush. Tell me what you have, and we will begin together."

Henri's fingers hovered above her papers, not yet touching them, acknowledging the weight they carried. Around them, the hall still churned with stamping, coughing, and muttered arguments, but at his desk, a stillness formed—a small, deliberate circle of peace.

Her shoulders eased as she explained—the small stove that barely warmed her rooms, the landlord's impatience, the silence in her classroom without Luc's violin to greet her in the evenings.

Henri guided her through each form with patient hands. His pen moved steadily, his voice low but certain. When her words faltered, he gave her silence instead of censure. Once, when her composure broke entirely, he slid a handkerchief across the desk without a word, lowering his eyes so she could gather herself in dignity.

At one point, Éloïse's gaze flicked toward *l'ouvrage* propped against the wall. The parrot's head tilted faintly, listening. She said nothing, but something in her expression softened, and she sensed she was not alone in the work of this morning.

By the time the last signature was set, her breathing had steadied, and she tied the ribbon around the bundle once more.

"You have been kind, Monsieur Fournier," Éloïse said. Her voice was still hushed, but there was strength in it now. "Kinder than duty requires. Thank you."

Henri inclined his head. He did not trust himself to answer, but his hand brushed *l'ouvrage*, and it was warm with approval.

Éloïse Aubert rose, and for the first time in many months, she walked away from a desk in the Hôtel de Ville with a burden made just a bit lighter.

# LA CHAMBRE VIDE

*The Empty Room*

É loïse climbed the narrow stairs to her apartment, the ribbon-tied bundle pressed against her chest. The stairwell smelled of boiled cabbage and coal dust, of other lives layered above and below her own. She unlocked the door, stepped inside, and was met by a silence heavier than the walls themselves.

The little room still bore Luc's presence, preserved as though he might return at any moment. His violin rested in its case atop the wardrobe, bow tucked beside it. His jacket hung by the door, shoulders faintly bowed, remembering the man it once clothed. Even his shoes remained beneath the chair, soles cracked from years of walking the same streets with her.

She placed the bundle of papers on the table. For months, those forms had chained her to the Hôtel de Ville, the cruelest part of widowhood—not the grief, but the endless proof required of it. Today, at least, thanks to that clerk's unexpected kindness, that part was finished. The weight of signatures and refusals had lifted, leaving behind only the heavier weight of absence.

Her days were thinly stitched together: small meals of broth, the mending of hems, letters half written, abandoned. She had not taught since Luc's passing, and the hush of the schoolroom echoed here as well. Sometimes she read aloud from the Psalms just to hear a voice in the room, but even then, the words felt borrowed, not her own.

She passed her hand over the violin case, fingers grazing the worn leather. "Not yet," she whispered.

Since leaving the Hôtel de Ville, she had spoken to no one, and the quiet that followed her home was deeper than the rain.

Yet when she thought back on the morning, she remembered his eyes—not the sharp glare of the beaked-nose man, but the calm of the one who had stepped forward at the last. There had been something measured in his voice, a courage that stood against the rest of the room.

A knock broke her reverie: three soft raps at the door, ordinary as Sunday. Éloïse rose, smoothed her veil, and opened it. On the landing stood Madame Rousseau from across the hall, a basket of rolls balanced on her arm.

"I baked too many," she said simply, pressing one into Éloïse's hand before she could refuse.

The crust was still warm when Éloïse laid it on the table. She traced a hand across its ridges, surprised by how something so simple could change a room so much.

Madame Rousseau lingered in the doorway, arms crossed, as though reluctant to leave her alone.

"The children ask after you," she said at last. "They say the benches are too quiet without Madame Aubert. Even the headmaster admits it." A half-smile, half-reproach. "You are missed at the school, Éloïse."

Then, without thinking, she added, "Luc would have wanted you there. He said once that no classroom could hold its tune without you. You remember how he was."

The words came with a rueful smile, but as soon as they were spoken, she regretted them, lowering her eyes.

"Forgive me. I only mean—he was proud of you."

The name, and the memory of his music, struck Éloïse like a stone dropped in water—sharp at first, then rippling outward. *Luc.* She had not allowed herself to think of his songs, the melodies that had once threaded through their small rooms like a second heartbeat.

Now the hush was complete, broken only by Madame Rousseau's clumsy kindness.

Éloïse broke off a piece of the bread and ate slowly. It was only bread, and yet more than bread—a sign that life might be given back, not all at once, but in crusts and crumbs, in neighbors who remembered, in children who still waited, and even in the awkward utterance of a name that was hers to bear.

At last, she thanked Madame Rousseau and closed the door. The little apartment grew still again. In the corner leaned Luc's violin. Éloïse lifted it into her hands, cradling it against her. The wood was cool, the strings mute. She did not draw the bow. She only held it until the weight of memory pressed tears from her eyes, and she wept into the quiet.

# LA PLUIE
*The Rain*

Months passed, and nothing changed. Luc's violin still gathered dust in its corner, his coat still hung by the door, his shoes still waited.

Éloïse rose each morning, swept the same floorboards, mended what did not need mending. Meals were plain, taken without appetite. The days grew shorter, then longer again, but her life stayed fixed, quiet as stone.

At last, some small stirring—not hope, only necessity—drew her outside. She pulled on a dress too loose at the waist, pinned her hair without care, and went to the market.

The square was alive with color: apples polished like lanterns, herbs sharp with fragrance, fish glistening on beds of ice. She moved among them like a ghost, bartering with a weak voice, gathering a modest sack of bread, onions, and greens.

The first drop of rain struck her cheek before she had crossed the square. Then came another, and another—until the sky fell open. The crowd scattered, vanishing beneath awnings and doorways.

Éloïse searched for shelter, but every space was filled. She hurried toward home, clutching her bundle, the stones slick beneath her shoes.

As she stepped from the curb, her hem snagged on a cart wheel and tore. The sack slipped from her arms, spilling its contents into the mud. Apples rolled into the gutter, bruising as they went. Onions split open, their pale skins soaking up the filth. The loaf of bread lay sodden, dissolving where it fell. She dropped to her knees, scrabbling at the muck, hair plastered to her face, rain soaking her through until cold seeped into her bones.

At that moment, something inside Éloïse broke. She pressed her hands over her face and sobbed aloud—a sound raw enough to turn heads.

"Luc," she whispered into the storm, his name lost beneath the thunder of rain. Her dress clung heavy to her skin, her groceries ruined, her life shattered beyond mending. Everything—the years of music, the warmth of their bed, the certainty of his hand in hers—had dissolved, leaving only this: a woman alone in the street, undone by the weather.

And then—a break in the torrent. Stillness above her, though the rain still roared beyond.

Was she … *dry?*

An umbrella, black and wide, stretched over her. The air beneath the canopy changed—warmer, calmer—the storm held at bay not only from her skin, but from her heart. Her sobs eased without her willing it; the rain was no longer the only thing she carried.

A hand rested gently on her shoulder. "Madame," a quiet voice said.

She raised her face, streaming with tears and rain, and saw a man's figure beside her, blurred by the storm. Behind him waited a carriage, its lanterns glowing dim through the downpour.

"Shall I assist, Monsieur Fournier?" the driver called from his seat.

Éloïse gasped, unable to speak, and let herself be

lifted from the mud, guided toward the open coach.

# LE CAFÉ
*The Café*

T he coach carried them only a short distance, turning from the drenched market square onto a quiet street. Éloïse sat trembling, her dress still clinging close from the cold, though she was miraculously dry now, and not a drop of rain had touched her since he'd lifted the umbrella. Her hands, clasped in her lap, were warm—like the storm had never happened.

At last, she dared to glance at the man beside her, and said softly, "Monsieur Fournier."

It was the timid clerk she remembered from the Hôtel de Ville—the one who had spoken gently when others dismissed her. Then, he had been hardly more than a shadow behind a desk. Now, Henri sat upright, his hair and coat arranged with quiet care, his gaze steady and searching, though a trace of shyness lingered at the corners of his eyes.

When the carriage stopped, he offered his hand. "Come," he said simply.

She let him guide her down to the threshold of a small café, its windows fogged with warmth. Inside, the smell of coffee and fresh bread wrapped around her like a blanket.

The room was nearly empty, with only a pair of students bent over books in the corner. They took a table by the window, and a waiter brought a basket of rolls and steaming cups of coffee. Éloïse wrapped her hands around the porcelain, the heat sinking into her bones.

The words came unbidden.

She spoke of her quiet rooms, of Luc's shoes still waiting by the door, of the violin she could not bring herself to play. She told him how the days blurred together, how she had not found her way back to the school, how loneliness clung to her like a second skin. When she faltered, ashamed of having said too much, Henri only inclined his head; every word was worth hearing.

At last, she drew a breath and looked at him across the small table.

"And you, Monsieur Fournier? What of your life since then?"

He smiled faintly. "Please, call me Henri. It has been some time since that day at the Hôtel de Ville. I was … less certain of myself then." A pause. "I still am, often enough."

She studied him, surprised by the candor. "And yet, you found me in the storm."

His shoulders lifted in a modest shrug. "Providence and luck, madame. I have had … opportunities. Work that carries more responsibility. A title, perhaps—but only paper. I am still the same man." His tone held no boast.

Their cups cooled as they lingered. He asked about small things—whether she still walked by the chestnut trees near the river, if her neighbors were kind, if she had seen the children singing in the square. His voice was calm, gentle, never prying.

When the rain outside had thinned to a drizzle, Henri called for the coach again. They rode in silence back toward her quarter.

He glanced toward the window, where the droplets had begun to gather once more. "The rain hasn't finished," he said softly. Then, turning to her, he added, "This was entrusted to me—with words I was told never to forget."

He recited them slowly, reverently:

*"Pas à vendre. Pas à garder. Pour un cœur vrai."*

He set *l'ouvrage* in her lap—black silk, its handle carved in the shape of a parrot's head, lacquered and watchful.

For a moment, his eyes met hers with quiet gravity.

"I cannot accept this," she whispered.

"You can, and you must," insisted Henri. *"Pour un cœur vrai."*

She wanted to ask why, to ask what it meant, to ask why he had chosen her. But the words would not come.

She stepped from the carriage, still clutching *l'ouvrage*, and watched it roll away into the night.

She opened the gift for the short walk to her doorway. The canopy unfurled with a sigh, the parrot's head catching the lamplight. The cobblestones beneath her feet dried instantly, shining like polished glass.

She could have sworn she smelled iron and roses.

# LA MAISON RÉVEILLÉE
*The Awakened House*

That night, Éloïse lay in bed with *l'ouvrage* propped against the wall, the parrot's head catching stray glints of lamplight. She closed her eyes, but sleep would not come.

Outside, the storm rose—wind clawed at the shutters, rain pounded the panes, thunder shook the little house on its foundations. The night itself refused to let her rest.

She pressed her palms against her eyes, willing herself still. But the storm only grew louder. She buried her head in her pillow and sang nonsense into the mattress. But the storm only grew louder. She stared at the ceiling, the walls, the floors—and still the storm grew louder, calling her.

Finally, something within her answered—a pressure, a tightness she could no longer bear. At last, she flung off the coverlet. Her bare feet struck the floor like a decision.

She lit the fire. Sparks leapt, flames caught, shadows sprang to life. She lit her lamps one by one until every corner of the room glowed. Darkness owned the outside, but within her walls, there would be light.

Then she began to move.

She swept the floorboards, the bristles of the broom slapping the planks in staccato rhythm. She folded shawls, stacked papers long neglected, straightened chairs that had sat askew for months. She dragged the washtub forward, poured water, scrubbed linens until her arms ached, wrung them out, and hung them dripping by the fire. The scent of soap and smoke mingled—sharp, clean, alive.

Her pace quickened.

She pulled Luc's shoes from the doorway and carried them to the wardrobe, setting them side by side with deliberate care. She took his coat from its peg, brushed the dust from its sleeves, and laid it away.

Each act hurt. Each act healed.

She paused longest at the violin. She did not open the case, did not lift the bow, but she dusted it, smoothed the lid, and set it square on its stand, as though preparing the silence to receive music once more.

All through the night, the storm raged, thunder rolling like a drumbeat, rain lashing the roof like a tide. And all through the night, Éloïse worked. She swept, she folded, she scrubbed, she ordered, she restored. Each stroke of her broom, each folded garment, each cleared surface was a blow against the weight that had pressed her down. Her heart kept time with her hands until she could scarcely tell which was storm and which was her own release.

At last, the blackness of the windows thinned to gray. Dawn crept into the storm, and with it, the violence of the night began to weaken. Rain slowed to a whisper. Clouds tore open. The first pale shaft of light spilled across her newly ordered room, glinting off *l'ouvrage* where it leaned, silent witness to the night's labor.

Éloïse set down the broom. Her hair was damp with sweat, her arms ached, her body trembled with exhaustion. Yet her home was transformed—not new, not Luc's, but hers.

She opened the door. The air outside was clean, streets shining, gutters trickling. She stepped out with *l'ouvrage* in her hand. The parrot's head glinted in the morning light, and she rested her palm against it.

She walked farther than she had dared in many months—past the baker's shop with its bright shutters and the smell of bread drifting warm into the street; past the chestnut trees bejeweled with rain, each drop catching the light like glass; past sparrows shaking themselves dry in the eaves, their wings clapping in bursts. Colors sharpened—the red of shutters flung open to the day, the green sheen of leaves, the silver rush of water through the gutters. Sounds were crisp—the bell of a milk cart turning the corner, the creak of a window swinging wide, and the sudden burst of children's laughter as they splashed through puddles, their voices ringing like bells. The cool stones were firm beneath her steps, the brush of air clean against her cheek, the weight of *l'ouvrage* in her hand—not heavy, but sure, as though it tethered her to the morning itself.

At the corner of the square, she stopped. The sun broke free of the clouds, gilding the rooftops, striking her face with warmth. She closed her eyes, lifted her head, and let it bathe her.

And Éloïse—widow, mourner, keeper of silence—smiled.

# LE CHANT DES ENFANTS

*The Children's Song*

The knock at her door came early one morning. Éloïse wiped her hands on her apron and opened it to find the headmaster on the step, his hat dripping with last night's rain. He looked older than she remembered, his mustache grayer, but his eyes were kind.

"Madame Aubert," he said, bowing slightly. "It has been too long. The children ask after you every day. We have tried to manage, but the classroom is not the same without you."

Éloïse started to cry. She had expected reproach, pity, even dismissal—but not this gentleness.

The headmaster cleared his throat. "Would you consider returning? Not for me. For them. They miss you so."

"Oh…" The sound escaped her—half laugh, half sob. "Oh, yes. Yes, monsieur."

She threw her arms around him. The headmaster went rigid with shock—his hat tumbled to the doorstep—but Éloïse held on for one fierce moment before stepping back, laughing at his expression, at herself, at the sheer impossible gift of it.

"Forgive me, monsieur. Yes. Yes, I will come back."

She was smiling—truly smiling—and the headmaster smiled back.

When the morning bell rang, Éloïse stood before the door of the schoolhouse. The timbers smelled of musty chalk, just as they had the first day she had stepped inside as a young woman. She had been the new music teacher then, nervous with her stack of songbooks.

Luc had been there too—teaching arithmetic with a light and subtle manner. She had often caught him humming under his breath, the same melodies he would later draw from his violin in the quiet of their rooms. Their voices had met over the children's recitations, and before long, their lives had been joined as one.

Now she stood at that same threshold, heart pounding, breath shallow. She closed her eyes, pressed her hand to the parrot's head, and entered.

When the children saw her, an enormous cheer went up.

Benches scraped as they rushed forward, voices tumbling over one another—*"Madame! Madame!"* They clutched at her hands, her skirts, her sleeves, tugging her into the room with laughter. Some hugged her outright, their faces wet with tears, though she did not know if they were theirs or hers.

The headmaster raised his hand for quiet, but the children couldn't help themselves. Éloïse took her place at the front. For a moment, words failed her. Then she lifted a familiar book and tapped the cover.

"Let us begin with something we all remember."

Her voice was tentative at first as she hummed the opening of *"À la Claire Fontaine."*

The children answered—thin, uncertain—then gathered strength until the classroom filled with their song.

They moved from one to another—*"Au Clair de la Lune,"* *"Frère Jacques,"* even a psalm that Luc had once insisted she teach, his voice joining back then with a gravity that had made the children stand up straighter.

The music returned to her—to her breath, to her bones. The benches that had been pews of mourning now rang with laughter and clapping. Life was flowing again—through the room, and through her.

Then she noticed movement at the back. A small boy with dark hair and a scar along his brow was peeking in through the window, eyes wide, lips parted in wonder. He did not enter, only pressed his ears against the frame to get closer to the sound.

One of the older pupils whispered, "He only comes for the music, madame. Never for the lessons."

Éloïse looked toward the window once more. The boy's gaze met hers for the briefest moment before he slipped away, vanishing into the brightness outside.

She lingered where she stood, the children's voices rising around her, filling the room with song.

# LA MUSIQUE
*The Music*

Spring had come to Paris. The trees in the square were heavy with blossoms, their scent drifting through the open windows of Éloïse's home. She left the shutters wide, so the air carried both the perfume of lilacs and the distant sounds of the street—carriage wheels, vendors calling, the bells of Saint-Gervais.

On her table lay Luc's violin. For months, she had only dusted it, tended it, honored it in silence. Some mornings, she would pause beside it, her hand over the case, but she always turned away. *Not yet. Not yet.*

But it was spring now. The scent of flowers through the open window. The sound of children's voices rising from the square. The way light pooled across her floor in the evenings, warm and insistent.

One night, she found herself standing before the table longer than usual. The case sat there, patient, waiting. She traced the edge with one finger, then drew it slightly toward her, and stopped. Her heart was racing as she pulled out the chair and sat down. She stared at the case for a long moment—at the worn leather, the tarnished clasp. Luc's hands must have touched this clasp ten thousand times.

She opened it.

The wood gleamed in the failing light. The bow rested in its velvet groove, horsehair perfect. Luc had always kept it perfect.

Her hands trembled when she lifted the instrument.

It settled beneath her chin—familiar weight, familiar curve—and for a moment, she simply held it, breathing.

Then she drew the bow across the strings.

She played the songs she had taught the children—*"À la Claire Fontaine," "Frère Jacques"*—then others Luc had loved, melodies that had been his solace at the end of long days.

At last, she closed her eyes and let her own music pour forth—something that was not his, not theirs, but hers alone.

The room widened; the shadows thinned. When she finished, the silence that followed was not empty, but full.

Éloïse smiled.

In time, word spread. A neighbor asked if she might teach her daughter, who longed to hold the violin. Then another came, and soon Éloïse had a small circle of private pupils—children who gathered in her parlor with wide eyes and eager fingers. She guided their hands, corrected their posture, praised their courage when the strings squeaked. Their laughter filled the house, and with it came her own.

Each morning, she walked to the school, her place restored, her voice once more joining the children's. The streets shed their gray and shined with familiar light. Vendors greeted her by name, and she answered without hesitation. She had found her rhythm again—not the old one, but a new measure that was hers alone.

Always, *l'ouvrage* rested near—leaned against her chair as she taught, propped by the window as she played, carried lightly on her walks, its parrot's head watching like a silent guardian. She scarcely thought of it, yet she never set it far aside.

Sometimes, when the light caught the silk just so, she would think of the words—and let them pass through her like a half-remembered prayer:

*Pas à vendre. Pas à garder. Pour un cœur vrai.*

Éloïse blossomed.

LE SCÉLÉRAT
"The Scoundrel"
LIVRE IV

# LIVRE IV : LE SCÉLÉRAT

## LE MARCHAND
*The Shopkeeper*

They called him *Maître Marchand,* though he owned no true shop. His trade sprawled across a twisted stall beneath the arcades of Les Halles—a place where honest vendors sold onions and chestnuts, and less honest men found corners deep enough for deceit.

Once, Marchand had owned a proper shop—a real establishment with glass windows and his name painted proudly above the door. Marchand et Fils—"Marchand and Sons." The *et Fils* had been optimism, hope painted in gilt letters for the son who would inherit.

But his son had died before his third winter. His wife had followed within the year, her grief sharper than any fever.

He fought for the shop. Borrowed at terrible rates, pawned everything that wasn't bolted down, worked until his hands cramped and his eyes blurred. But you cannot pay debt with exhaustion. The creditors came anyway. They took it piece by piece, until even the gilt letters belonged to someone else.

What remained was this: a twisted stall beneath the arcades, a tarnished reputation, a small wooden sign hung above the stall, its letters long faded:

*Marchand & Fils*

*Curiosités et Fils de Rien*

The second line had begun as a jest and stayed as a truth: *"Curiosities and Sons of Nothing."*

So, while honest vendors sold onions and chestnuts, Marchand sold whatever could be moved quickly. Not because he lacked a conscience—though many thought he did—but because Paris had taken everything honest from him, and he would not let it take the rest.

To the unwary, he was genial, his voice rich and warm, his smile broad as charity. To those who knew him, that smile meant a hand reaching deeper into their purse.

He kept his stall in deliberate disorder—as though by accident—so that the passerby might feel clever for discovering a "treasure." He'd praise the customer's taste, press their hand in mock gratitude, then send them away with a trinket worth a fraction of what they'd paid. His wares: ribbons dyed too bright, clocks whose hands never agreed, bottles of wine thinned with water and sweetened again with syrup.

Paris had many such dealers, but Marchand thrived by appearing harmless.

He was not.

Boys worked for him by the dozen—ragged, hungry, nameless. They ran errands, fetched parcels, carried messages, shouted bargains into the crowd. He paid them in crusts, in coins so light they slipped through their fingers, in promises that evaporated by morning.

Among them was one quieter than the rest, dark-haired, with a faint scar across his brow. Marchand never used his name—he never used anyone's—only whistles or

86

the snap of his fingers. Yet the boy watched him closely. While the others jostled and called, he listened—to the lies, to the laughter, to the small, sharp ways the world could be twisted.

"Keep your eyes open," Marchand would say, cuffing whichever child was nearest. "News is worth more than bread." And so, they learned to watch: which carts came from Rouen, which casks were spoiled, which housewives carried too much coin.

When it rained, Marchand worked the crowd from beneath his awning, wine glass in hand, his stall dripping at the edges. He liked the rain; it made people hurry and forget their change. The rain pooled in the hollows of his counter, reflecting his face in crooked fragments. He grinned at the image, raised his glass in mock salute, and drank.

Paris might wash itself clean each night, but *Maître Marchand* always found the dirt again by morning.

# LE MARCHAND ET L'OUVRAGE

*The Shopkeeper and the Masterpiece*

The morning was bright after rain, the stones of Les Halles still slick, the air rich with the scent of onions, smoke, and salt. Éloïse came with her basket, *l'ouvrage* in her hand. Habit, perhaps—or instinct. Children trailed beside her, one clutching a coin for sweetmeats, another humming the song they had sung that week.

Marchand saw her before she saw him.

His stall crouched beneath the arcades, draped with ribbons and trinkets, clocks that ticked unevenly. He leaned against a timber post, eyes narrowing, smile already fixed.

"Ah, Madame Aubert," he called, loud enough for the market to hear. "You have something that belongs to me."

Éloïse stopped. "I beg your pardon?"

Marchand stepped forward, his tone sharpening. "That umbrella. Black silk, lacquered parrot's head. It was stolen from me some time ago."

Éloïse's voice was steady, though astonished. "You are mistaken, *monsieur*. This was entrusted to me. A gift. It is not yours."

"'Entrusted'?" He gave a short, dry laugh. "A fine word for stolen goods."

At a whistle, two of his boys appeared—ragged, thin, eyes downcast. "You remember," Marchand pressed, resting a heavy hand on one lad's shoulder. "Was this not my property?"

The boys nodded, their voices small, rehearsed—but in the noise of Les Halles, even small lies could sound like truth.

A guard approached, drawn by the quarrel. "What's this, then?"

"A trifle," Marchand said smoothly. "Merchandise stolen long ago, now found again."

Éloïse clutched *l'ouvrage* tighter. "This man lies! It was given to me, by a friend."

The guard looked from one to the other, then at the object itself. "If there's dispute," he said, "the dealer's claim stands until proof is shown. Do you have papers, madame?"

Éloïse faltered. Papers? For a gift sealed by trust, spoken from the heart? She shook her head.

Marchand's smile widened. He plucked *l'ouvrage* from her grasp with a mock bow. "Then let us call it settled."

Éloïse pleaded, "This is outrageous!"

The guard muttered in reply, "Best leave it, madame. It's only an umbrella." Then he was gone.

For an instant, as his hand closed on the handle, Marchand felt something inside. The carved parrot regarded him—not with judgment, but with patience. The silk beneath his fingers carried warmth that had nothing to do with the sun.

A thought surfaced, small and unwelcome:

*You could give it back.*

*You could apologize, return it to the widow, walk away.*

But debt makes cowards of honest men and thieves of cowards. He thought of the creditors circling, the rent overdue, the empty frame where his family's likeness once sat before he'd pawned even that.

His hand tightened on the shaft.

"Thank you, madame," he said to the widow's retreating back, mocking. The words tasted of ash. "Your honesty is appreciated."

The umbrella grew heavier in his grip. The warmth faded to ice cold.

Marchand turned, strutting through the stalls, *l'ouvrage* tucked beneath his arm as though it had always been his. The boys trailed behind—one jeering, one silent, and the dark-haired one with the scar glancing back, his expression unreadable.

Éloïse stood in the square, her students silent now, the weight of loss again pressing heavier than lead.

They walked back to the school without singing.

That evening, as the lamps were being lit, she went to the Hôtel de Ville. Henri received her in his small office, his eyes grave as she told the story. He listened without interruption, then at last shook his head.

"I can enter your protest," he said quietly, "but it will not change what the guard has written. The record will favor him now. Unless the thing itself returns, the papers are stronger than truth."

Éloïse bowed her head. His voice was kind—but final. *L'ouvrage* was gone. Stolen by a scoundrel.

She left the bureau as night fell, her steps echoing on the stones, the city loud around her. The rain began

again, and the gutters began to sing—a sad, thin music
that no one else seemed to hear.

# L'OUVRAGE VOLÉ

*The Stolen Masterpiece*

For a week, Marchand strutted through Les Halles with *l'ouvrage* tucked beneath his arm. The silk glinted in the sun, the parrot's head bobbing above the crowd. He carried it not for shelter—the days were bright—but for show. Each time he lifted it, he smirked, certain the stallholders watched with envy.

"Fine silk!" he called. "Parisian craft, rare as gold! Worth more than a month's rent!" He twirled it like a *bâton*, laughed, and leaned it against his stall so all might see it standing guard over his crooked wares.

But already, there were signs.

The boys noticed first. They whispered that when Marchand lifted it in the rain, the drops found him anyway—sliding under the canopy, soaking his collar, dampening his sleeves. He shouted and cuffed them for laughing, but still they whispered.

There were other signs as well. The canopy caught on its own ribs, refusing to open smoothly. The lacquered handle was always colder than the day allowed, its sheen dulled as though the light itself withdrew. Marchand cursed and struck it against the post, but no amount of polish restored the gleam.

The boy with the scar watched in silence.

Once, at Marchand's command, he had fetched the umbrella from across the square. The sky was clear, yet the weight of it felt different in his hand—not heavy, but alive, almost trembling. For a moment, the handle warmed beneath his fingers, and the silk stirred. He did not understand it, only that the strangeness felt right— and that it frightened him a little. When Marchand shouted for it back, he had hesitated before returning it, the loss sharper than he expected.

Marchand, blind to the warnings, strutted and shouted louder. He boasted of his clever bargain, waving the black silk to draw customers, but those who came near lingered only briefly. Their eyes flicked toward the umbrella, then away, uneasy. The stall, once noisy, grew strangely still.

By dusk, the air had soured. The usual market smells—bread, smoke, fish—twisted into something wrong. A faint stench of sulfur and ash clung to March- and's stall, though no fires burned nearby. Flies gathered, though nothing rotted there. The cobbles beneath his feet were slick with the day's refuse. He wiped his brow and found it wet.

Beside him, the umbrella leaned in silence, the par- rot's head shining faintly, its gaze too watchful.

# LES GARÇONS DE LA HALLE

*The Market Boys*

Marchand never lacked for boys to do his bidding. They came hungry, with eyes sharp and ribs showing through their shirts, willing to carry any parcel for a crust. He used them as he used his scales—tilted always in his favor. A coin for a day's running, two if the errand was long. More often, nothing at all but a cuff on the ear and the promise of "next time."

The boys knew it, yet they lingered. He gave them scraps from the stall, let them sip watered wine, taught them curses to make the crowd laugh. And sometimes he boasted of his umbrella—the black silk with the parrot's head—as a banner they marched beneath.

But the banner failed them. When the rain came sudden and hard, the boys huddled under its canopy, only to find themselves drenched all the same. Water ran down their backs, filled their shoes, plastered their hair.

Marchand roared with laughter, calling them fools for pressing too close—though he was soaked through himself. His laughter rang thin, brittle, like cracked glass.

Word spread quickly through Les Halles. Housewives whispered that his ribbons stained their fingers, that his clocks stopped within the week, that his bottles soured before they were opened. True or not, the gossip stuck. His customers dwindled. Men who once lingered for a bargain now crossed the street instead.

Then the creditors began to appear. A butcher

demanded coin for meat never paid for, a carter for transport never settled. Marchand swore, shouted, waved the umbrella like a weapon—but the men only smirked and walked away. His stall grew quieter by the day.

The boys, too, drifted off. One by one, they vanished, gone to better work—a baker's apprentice, a porter's helper, even a washerwoman's errand boy paid in bread. By midsummer, only a few remained—the desperate, and one who watched with different eyes.

The boy with the scar.

Marchand sat alone often then, chin in his hand, eyes fixed not on his wares, but on nothing at all. The umbrella leaned beside him, its silk dulled, the parrot's head swallowed by shadow. He stroked it sometimes, as though it might comfort him, but his hand always fell away. It gave no warmth.

The boy noticed. He saw how Marchand's boasts had thinned to mutters, how his laughter had turned to silence, how in the evenings, he lingered at the edge of the market with a look that was not greed, but weariness—the look of a man who held something precious and found it empty in his hands.

And he understood. For Marchand, *l'ouvrage* was no prize. It was judgment.

# LA MISE EN GAGE
*The Pawning*

By late summer, Marchand's stall sagged like his shoulders. The wares were fewer, the colors duller, the laughter gone. He had pawned half of it already—a clock here, a crate of ribbons there—and still the creditors muttered at his back.

One evening, when the market thinned to shadows, he lifted *l'ouvrage* and held it close. The silk drooped in his grip, the parrot's head dull, lifeless.

"Enough," he muttered. "You will fetch a price, at least."

He crossed the square to a pawnbroker's window—a place he knew well, where everything was trapped behind glass: watches, candlesticks, silver spoons, their gleam turned cold.

The broker, a small man with eyes like coins, raised an eyebrow at the umbrella, turned it once, twice.

"Fine work," he said, without regard. "But no one pays for shelter on a sunny day. Five francs."

*"Five?"* Marchand barked. "Silk like this is worth twenty, at least!"

The broker set it down without ceremony. "For a man with choices, perhaps. I offer five."

Marchand's jaw tightened. His hand clenched the parrot's head until his knuckles blanched. The lacquer was colder than glass, the silk dull beneath his thumb—dead weight. He slammed it down on the counter.

A whiff of sulfur and ash rose from the fabric, faint but unmistakable.

"Take it," he spat. "It's brought me nothing but grief."

The broker laughed softly, wrote a slip, and pushed the coins forward.

The small boy with the scar, waiting by the door with a parcel in his arms, saw the moment. He saw the umbrella pass across the counter—and with it, something more: the last shred of Marchand's pride.

When he stepped back into the street, Marchand's pockets jingled faintly, but his shoulders sagged lower than ever. "Five francs," he muttered again and again.

Behind the glass, *l'ouvrage* leaned in the shadows, silk folded, the parrot's painted eye reflecting the lamplight—patient, watchful, waiting.

# LA CHUTE DU MARCHAND

*The Fall of the Shopkeeper*

That night, Marchand sat alone beneath the arcades. His stall was bare—little more than a twisted table and a sagging cloth. The boys were gone. The customers were gone. Even the creditors were gone, having judged him empty.

In his pocket clinked the five francs from the pawnshop—five thin coins, lighter than air, heavier than shame. He turned them in his palm, as though they might grow more valuable with motion.

They did not.

The rain began, soft at first, then harder.

He lifted no canopy. He had nothing left to lift. Water soaked his collar, ran down his cheeks, mingled with the salt of his own bitterness.

The rain was cold and filthy, and it tasted of ash. It ran gray down the gutters, carrying the day's refuse. A rat emerged from beneath his table, paused, then scurried past.

He thought of the black silk, of the parrot's head that had once sparkled like a promise. He had boasted of it, strutted with it, held it high as proof of his cleverness. And in the end, it had left him poorer than before—stripped, small, forgotten.

Somewhere beyond the market, thunder rolled. The gutters filled. In the pawnbroker's window across the square, a faint gleam of black silk caught the lightning and was gone.

By midnight, Les Halles stood empty but for him—a hunched figure in the rain, muttering to no one.

Through the far end of the arcade, a tall man walked, unhurried, coat dry, though the rain poured down. His steps made no sound on the stones. The water parted around him, then closed in again.

He did not look at Marchand, nor pause, nor speak. He simply passed—and Marchand felt winter move through him.

When at last he rose and left the stall behind, no one marked his going.

By morning, only his debts remained.

Thunder cracks overhead—close enough to rattle the bottles behind the bar, to make the lamplight shudder. Someone near the door mutters a prayer. You glance toward the window, rain streaming down the glass, then back at me.

You're quiet now. Around us, voices have dropped to murmurs.

I know what you're thinking: *Must everyone who touches it suffer?*

Not suffer. Be tested.

There's a difference, though it's a fine one.

LE POLICIER
"The Policeman"
LIVRE V

# LIVRE V:
# LE POLICIER

## CAPITAINE GIRARD
*Captain Girard*

The pawnbroker's shop smelled of dust and metal—watches stacked like hoarded time, candlesticks dulled with neglect, silver spoons gone gray in the shadows. Behind the counter, *l'ouvrage* leaned among them, silk folded, its parrot's head peering through the glass, a captive bird.

The door opened with a jangle of bells.

A man filled the threshold—broad-shouldered, red-faced. Ornate brass buttons, clunky and garish, gleamed on his long captain's coat, giving him the look of a toy soldier past his prime. A cigarette hung from his teeth, its ember flaring each time he drew breath, casting red flashes across his damp face. At his belt swung a short *bâton* that tapped against his thigh as he walked.

"Inspection," he barked.

The broker nodded, shuffling papers.

Girard moved through the narrow aisles, tapping ledgers with a thick finger, prodding the stacks of pawned lives. Then his eye caught the umbrella. He bent, lifted it, and turned it once in his hands.

"Fine piece," he said. "What's its record?"

"Pawned yesterday evening," the broker replied. "Five francs only. But…" He twisted the shaft just below the runner, where the brass collar met the wood. A faint sigil glinted in the lamplight. "It bears a maker's mark."

Girard leaned closer, breath sour, eyes narrowing. He traced the stamp with a finger. "Guillaume," he said, low and certain. "His hand is known. This is worth far more than five francs."

He snapped the canopy shut with a crack that made the broker flinch. "Plainly stolen property," he said. "There will be an inquiry." His tone suggested that the outcome was already written.

The broker spread his hands—a smile half pleading, half servile. "As you wish, Capitaine Girard. You've always had an eye for justice."

Girard grunted—whether in agreement or warning, it was hard to tell—and strode out into the street with *l'ouvrage* tucked under his arm, his gait stiff with authority, his face set in the grim assurance of duty performed.

The street beyond reeked of tanneries and standing water. Shadows pooled thick in doorways, despite the afternoon sun. A beggar slumped against the pawnbroker's wall, unmoving—asleep, drunk, or worse.

Girard stepped past without looking.

But the day was close and heavy, and despite the glare of the sun, the umbrella was cold in his grip. He shifted it once, frowning, then lit another cigarette and walked on.

# LE QUARTIER

*The Quarter*

As usual, Capitaine Girard walked the Marais like it belonged to him. His boots struck the stones in cadence, shoulders squared, chin lifted. He carried *l'ouvrage* by the shaft, silk folded tight, the parrot's head forward in his grip. It glittered under the lanterns like an unblinking eye—or the iron head of a mace. In his hand, it was no shelter from rain, but a weapon, a symbol of command.

The Marais knew when Capitaine Girard was near. His boots marked a rhythm that carried ahead of him like a watchman's bell. Before he turned a corner, shutters drew to, laughter softened, and quarrels found their end. A cart driver hushed his mule with a glance at the approaching shadow. Fishmongers, midway through a curse, let the words die in their throats. Even the taverns dimmed, voices falling to whispers beneath the clink of glass. Most of the time, by the time Girard arrived, order had already preceded him.

He rarely needed to speak. And when he did, it was too late.

Children, too, knew that shadow. They listened for the cadence of those boots.

In the square before Saint-Paul-Saint-Louis, a knot of ragged boys jostled a woman's basket, snatching at her loaves. At the first glimpse of Girard, they scattered like pigeons startled from the stones. One stumbled and fell at his feet, a stolen crust skidding across the wet cobblestones. The boy clawed it up again and froze, crouched before the captain, hunger in his eyes and terror in his trembling hands.

The woman clutched what bread remained and turned toward Girard, expecting justice. His grip tightened on the umbrella's shaft, the parrot's head gleaming in the streetlights. Reflex urged him forward: to seize, to cuff, to make an example. For an instant, he raised *l'ouvrage*, the boy flinching beneath its shadow. Then, with effort, he let the breath out of his chest and lowered it.

Instead, he stooped, took the boy by the shoulder, and set him upright. "Go," he said—nothing more.

The child hesitated, then ran. Girard steadied the woman's basket, drew her shawl about her shoulders, and sent her on her way. She murmured thanks, though her eyes stayed wary, unsettled by the absence of the blow she had expected.

Rain began to spit—fat drops freckling the stones, darkening his coat. He did not open the umbrella. Removing his hat, he stood bare-headed in the drizzle, letting it streak his face, soak his collar. His authority was shelter enough.

Yet even as he marched on, boots drumming their rhythm through the narrow streets, a thought clung to him like the damp: for the first time in years, he had chosen not to strike. And that choice weighed heavier than any order he had barked that night.

# LA MAISON VIDE

*The Quiet House*

Capitaine Girard's apartment sat above a bakery on Rue Saint-Antoine. By day, the air smelled of bread and yeast, warm and sweet; by night, it was only flour dust and silence. The narrow stairs groaned beneath his boots—the kind that remembered every weight, but never welcomed it.

The rooms were squared like barracks, furnished with the barest necessities. A table with two chairs, though only one was ever used. A narrow iron bed, its coverlet folded with military precision. Shelves lined with ledgers and old orders, and beside them, a small dish of brass captain's buttons, their shine long since gone. Everything was clean, orderly—shaped by duty, not comfort.

On the chair by the door rested *l'ouvrage*, its black silk devouring the lamplight, an intruder too fine for the spartan room. Officially, he should have logged it as evidence. Officially, he should have done a lot of things.

On the mantel stood a single photograph in a frame of dark wood. The picture had faded, its edges curling, but the image endured: a young man in dress uniform, his coat cut long, ornate, oversized brass buttons gleaming even through the blur of age. His posture was proud, his smile uncertain.

Girard regarded the photo with pride and sadness, lingering, as one touches a wound: with recognition, but without indulgence.

There had been warmth here once. A table with

four chairs. A boy with dark hair stealing rolls before supper, his mother scolding gently. Laughter that filled these rooms like light.

The boy grew. The laughter faded. He spoke of duty, of honor, of a war that had already taken too many. Girard had tried to stop him: "You are not ready."

But the boy's answer was quiet and final: "I am already gone."

The letter came in spring. Brief, creased, smudged. After that, the house fell silent.

After that, everything changed.

Girard had sewn the brass buttons from the boy's uniform onto his own coat—a silent promise to carry his memory where duty once lived. But on the streets, he hardened. The badge lost its promise; the *bâton* found its purpose. He saw himself striking without thought: the Marais, Les Halles, Place Pigalle. The boy with the scar— the crack, the blood—a child marked forever by his hand.

The memory jolted him back, his mouth dry, the taste of ash on his tongue.

He lit the lamp with a grunt. Shadows spread across the walls.

He poured brandy, swallowed it, then poured again and left the glass untouched on the table. The bakery below had gone dark. Only the scrape of his boots, the creak of the chair, and the slow beat of his heart disturbed the air.

The silence was broken by a small sound—silk on wood. *L'ouvrage* had shifted in its spot by the door. Girard hesitated, then turned and lifted it, then opened it with a snap. Though the ceiling was low, he stood beneath the canopy.

The hush inside startled him. For a moment, the world outside fell away. Within that circle of silk was a stillness unlike any he had known in years.

He closed his eyes, and he could hear them: small feet across the boards, the rustle of skirts, voices that once filled these rooms. For a heartbeat, the quiet beneath the canopy was not empty, but alive.

Thunder pealed, and the spell broke. The room returned—bare, hollow, waiting. He snapped the canopy shut and leaned it back against the chair, unsettled.

Girard sat again, heavy hands clasped, eyes fixed on the lamplight. The hush lingered—not in the room now, but within him.

The boards creaked; the clock ticked; no ease came.

Midnight passed. The bells marked the hour. He only sat in the glow of the dying lamp, the hush within him holding fast—waiting for rain.

# L'ÉPREUVE
*The Trial*

He did not sleep.

By the small hours, he was pacing again, footsteps whispering over the boards, the untouched brandy glinting on the table.

Before the first light reached the shutters, he pulled on his boots and the familiar weight of his uniform. The bakery below had already stirred to life—the thump of dough, the scrape of baker's peels against stone, a door creaking open to the street. Habit carried him down the groaning stairs and out to Rue Saint-Antoine.

The Marais at dawn was not yet crowded, but it was no longer still. Bakers' boys hurried with baskets; market carts rattled toward the halls; a woman with a child at her hip waited beneath a doorway's narrow shelter. The air had that charged stillness Paris knows before a squall— breath held, sky the color of lead.

Girard quickened his step.

The first gust came like a shove. Canvas awnings snapped. A sign clattered loose. Rain followed in a sudden sheet, sharp enough to make people cry out. A cart hit a rut and lurched, and a crate of apples burst across the stones. The mare reared, harness bells frantic.

Girard stepped into the street, voice cutting through the wind. *"Du calme!"* he barked, one hand raised, the other gripping *l'ouvrage* by the shaft, the parrot's head thrust forward like a beacon. He steadied the horse, righted the cart, sent the driver on.

Another blast of rain drove at him, stinging his face, soaking his collar. Without thinking, he snapped the umbrella open above his head.

The torrent dulled at once; the heaviest drops veered from the silk. Yet a fine mist still found him—chill against his cheeks, damp at his neck. He frowned, lowering the canopy. The shelter held, but thinly, as *l'ouvrage* weighed his worth.

Then came a cry.

At the edge of the square, a young mother huddled with her child beneath a useless shawl. The wind tore at the little one's cap; the child's mouth was open in a silent wail. Girard took two strides, then three, and lifted *l'ouvrage* over them.

The change was immediate.

The rain's roar retreated. The air beneath the silk went still—warm as breath. The mother's shoulders dropped; she looked up, startled, meeting his gaze with gratitude he had not seen in years. The child hiccupped once, blinking at the sudden calm.

He stood with them a moment longer than duty required. Something loosened inside him. *"Par ici,"* he said quietly, guiding them to a recessed doorway. *"Restez."* She nodded, whispering thanks he pretended not to hear.

Across the square, a knot of boys crouched in the open—thin shoulders hunched, clothes plastered to their ribs. Each gust drove them back. Girard strode out, umbrella high. *"Par ici!"* he called.

They hesitated, then stumbled toward him. The first ducked under the canopy—then a second, a third, a fourth. It should have been too small, yet the silk stretched impossibly, making room. Soon they all huddled beneath it, dry as hearthstones.

Their eyes lifted, wary and wide. One boy stood apart—older by a year perhaps, dark hair plastered to his brow, a pale scar along his temple. His gaze fixed on Girard, cautious but unflinching.

Girard steeled himself. *"On y va,"* he said, and steered them through the flooded square, his free hand steadying the smallest as *l'ouvrage* tilted to shield them from the gale. Beyond the canopy was only noise, water, and the color of old coins. Beneath the silk was calm and dry—their breath quick but sure, their footsteps hushed.

They reached the arcade by Saint-Paul-Saint-Louis, its stonework streaming. Girard ushered them into the dry, counting without meaning to. They jostled and laughed nervously, shaking off their fear like wet dogs.

But the square was still chaos.

Girard raised *l'ouvrage* again and strode back into the torrent. He gathered the young mother and child first, then the porters straining against their cart, then a laundress whose basket had spilled into the gutter. Each time he opened the canopy over another soul, the storm recoiled, breaking against the black silk like surf on stone.

The arcade filled: mothers, boys, tradesmen—all blinking at one another, dry and safe, speaking in low, astonished tones.

By the time Girard turned back for the last time, the square was empty, its stalls overturned, apples bobbing in the gutters like small red boats. He guided the final stragglers—two girls no older than twelve—into the shelter, then lowered the umbrella. His coat hung heavy with rain, but everyone beneath the archways stood dry as noon.

One by one, they slipped away, back into the dripping streets as the storm broke apart.

At last, only the boys remained—and then they, too, scattered, their laughter fading down the alleys until only one was left.

The boy with the scar.

The rain softened to a whisper. Girard lowered himself onto the cold stone steps, his weight settling with a grunt. The boy lingered a few feet away, wary but unmoving, his eyes fixed on the captain. Neither spoke.

The bells of Saint-Paul rang the hour, clear and insistent. The boy flinched, but did not look away. Girard's hand tightened on the shaft of *l'ouvrage*, its silk faintly stirring in the wind.

The silence stretched.

For reasons neither understood, they remained there together, the storm thinning around them, until the square was empty.

Through the far end of the arcade, a figure passed— tall, unhurried, coat and hat dry despite the dripping stones. His steps made no sound.

Neither Girard nor the boy turned to look, but Paris took notice.

Then he was gone, and only the gutters sang.

# LA TRANSMISSION
*The Passing*

The square beyond the arcade lay strewn with broken stalls and bruised fruit, but beneath the stone, there remained only the captain, the boy, and the hush that clung to the black umbrella between them.

Girard's jaw worked. He stared at the wet stone at his feet, unable to meet the boy's eyes. His hand flexed on the shaft of *l'ouvrage*, then tightened again.

When he spoke, his voice was low, broken.

"I remember you," he said. "Place Pigalle."

He paused, touching his forehead. "I've carried it as long as you have." His eyes lowered. "Perhaps differently."

The words scraped out of him, rough and reluctant. He kept his gaze lowered—the boy's eyes were more than he could bear.

Silence stretched. Only the drip of water from the eaves filled it.

At last Girard drew a long breath. He turned *l'ouvrage* slowly, lowering the parrot's head toward the boy.

"It was never mine," he said, softer now.

Julien did not move at first. His dark hair clung to his brow, the pale scar bright against his skin. Then, cautiously, he reached out and closed his fingers around the shaft.

The silk stirred.

The scent of iron and roses struck them both.

Girard's hand lingered a heartbeat longer before slipping free. His shoulders eased; the weight gone from his palm left his chest strangely light. He still did not look up.

Julien rose, *l'ouvrage* folded in his grasp. He gave no thanks, no word at all—only a glance that was not fear, but recognition. Then he turned and slipped from the arcade, careful on the wet stones, the umbrella held close.

Girard watched him vanish into the dripping alleys until even the sound of his steps was gone.

The rain fell softer then, the last of the storm washing through the gutters. The captain stood alone, his hand empty, his heart at rest.

# LE DÉPART

*The Departure*

Morning light cut through the thinning storm, pale and cold on the cobblestones. The arcade stood empty now. Girard sat for a while until the sun had turned the storm to steam. Finally, he rose from the steps, knees stiff, and turned toward the station.

The walk was heavy. Each stride carried the weight of years—the barks and shoves, the nights of drink, the blows struck more easily than words. His boots, once the terror of the quarter, dragged as he crossed the square.

The station smelled of damp wool and concrete. The desk sergeant looked up, startled by the captain's presence, but Girard did not stop. He passed through the lobby into the narrow office that had been his for years.

Inside, nothing had changed: the scarred desk, the worn chair, the ledgers stacked in their strict rows. He unpinned the badge from his breast. The metal snapped free, leaving the cloth bare. For years, it had made his word law. Now it was only brass. He set it on the blotter.

Then he drew out the *bâton*. The wood was dark with sweat and age, polished where his hand had gripped it, scarred where it had struck.

They had called it a symbol of order. He knew better.

He laid it beside the badge.

For a long moment, he stood still.

Then, with purpose, he reached into his pocket for his knife. The click of the blade sounded loud in the small room. One by one, he cut the buttons from his coat, each coming free with a small tearing of thread. He placed them gently in his palm, feeling their weight, their warmth. Then he slipped them into his pocket.

At last, he shrugged off the uniform jacket and left it draped over the chair. From a hook by the door, he took down his civilian coat and pulled it on, lighter.

He stood a moment at the threshold, then turned the handle. Behind him, the badge, the *bâton*, and the uniform remained.

In the street, the city was washed clean from the storm. The bells of Saint-Paul carried faintly across the quarter, their notes bright as glass. Girard walked on, the buttons in his pocket clinking softly with each step.

He did not look back.

L'ORPHELIN
"The Orphan"
LIVRE VI

# LIVRE VI :
# L'ORPHELIN

## LE JOUR DE SAINT-JULIEN
*The Day of Saint Julien*

Paris slept beneath the rain.

A woman hurried through the alleys of the Marais, shawl clutched close, an infant pressed against her chest. His thin wails pierced the dark, each cry ricocheting off shuttered windows. To calm him, she hummed—low, broken at first, then steadier—a simple tune, almost a lullaby. The sound trembled with her grief, yet the child's cries softened, soothed by a music he would never remember and never forget.

It rocked in five notes, cradled close: a low note, then a higher one she held like a bell, back to low, a quick lift above, then home again, the bell-note lingering just long enough. Soft and sure, it went:

*do—sōōō—si—ré—do.*

Beautiful. Haunting.

Her shoes slapped the stones, water soaking through worn leather. She passed the iron gates of Saint-Paul, the square before the Hôtel de Ville, the market stalls standing like sentries. The rain blurred her eyes, but she did not stop until she reached the wall of the L'Hospice des Enfants-Trouvés, Rue d'Enfer. There, built into the stone, was *la roue*—the wheel: a wooden drum that turned on its axis, divided to hold what was given and conceal what was lost.

Shame and mercy, carved into one contrivance.

She laid the child inside, wrapped the cloth tighter, and bent close. For a long moment, she did not move. She kissed the boy's brow, pressed her cheek against his, and whispered something only he could hear—words that dissolved into the rain.

She hummed it once more, the same five-note cradle:

*do—sōōō—si—ré—do.*

The boy cooed.

At last, she turned the wheel. It creaked, pivoted, and the child was carried inward. She placed her hand once against the stone, then fled into the storm, the tune still echoing faintly in her ears.

Inside, the bell rang as the wheel completed its turn. Sister Agnès, on duty at the reception hearth, rose from her stool and opened the hatch. The bundle slid toward her, damp and trembling. She lifted the child into her arms, rocked him gently, and crossed herself.

By morning, the ledger waited open on the small desk. A timid young clerk arrived—shoulders narrow, his suit too large, fingers stained with ink. He bent low over the page, as though hiding from the very letters he formed.

The infant lay swaddled beside Sister Agnès's chair, half dozing after milk. The clerk glanced at him only once before turning his eyes toward the wall calendar. The day was marked in red: *Saint Julien.*

He touched the line lightly with his finger, then dipped the nib.

He wrote the name with care:

### Julien

Beneath it, in the column where a family should have stood, he wrote only:

*Orphelin, sans demeure;*
*note: hospice (Le jour de la St-Julien)*


The book closed with a soft thud. The child stirred, but did not wake.

Outside, the rain tapped against the stone walls, and Paris kept time.

# LA RUE

*The Street*

His first years belonged to the hospice. The walls were high, the corridors long, and the air always smelled faintly of soap and boiled milk. Rows of cots lined the nursery hall, each with a number more certain than a name. Sisters moved between them like shadows—murmuring prayers, ladling broth, smoothing blankets.

He was not unloved. The sisters were brisk, but kind. A kiss on the brow at night, a lullaby hummed absently— fragments of care, enough to keep him alive.

But the wheel gave many, and the hospice could not hold them all.

The days fell into order. Bells marked them: *Prime* for prayers, *Terce* for lessons, *Sext* for soup. Julien listened more than the others, their tones less command than comfort, each note a thread in the only song he knew by heart. A slate, a stub of chalk, letters copied until the board was gray with dust. He traced his name, though the letters weren't his:

*Julien*

A saint's name, not a mother's. He pressed his finger into the chalk to rub it away.

The older boys taught him more than the sisters did—how to slip bread from the kitchen when the trays were cooling, how to feign sickness and win an hour's rest in the laundry loft, how to fight without drawing blood. He learned all of it, but said little. Silence was safer than cleverness.

Nights were the hardest. Rows of children breathing in the dark, some crying softly, some whispering to mothers they still imagined would return. Julien never cried. Instead, he lay awake, listening—to the bells, to the scrape of carts beyond the wall, to the footsteps of sisters on stone. When Sister Agnès hummed over the cots, he listened with his whole body, as though the sound might fill what fate had left empty.

At ten, his turn came. A cooper took him for work—a dour man with thick wrists who smelled of oak and pitch. The shop was dim and hot, and the staves were heavy for a boy so slight. He lasted a season, no more. His hands blistered, his back bent, and when he faltered, the man cuffed him hard. Julien left without permission one night, slipping into the alleys of the Marais, where the hospice bell could no longer protect him.

From then on, the city became his roof.

His first nights were the hardest. He learned which doorsteps stayed dry, which market awnings could shield him from the rain, and how to wake at the faintest sound of boots on stone. Hunger drove him to the stalls— bruised apples dropped in haste, bread gone stale, bones gnawed and cast aside. He took whatever he could, quick as a rat, and ran when hands reached for him.

He grew leaner, sharper. The alleys taught him to keep still as stone when danger passed, to blend with the shadows—to disappear. His silence deepened; words were a luxury, wasted when bread was dearer.

In the streets, he hunted for music as surely as for food. A fiddler at a corner, an organ-grinder with his

monkey, a woman singing to herself as she hung washing—he lingered for such sounds, hiding nearby until
the last note faded. Sometimes he crept close to the little
schoolhouse on Rue des Martyrs, pressing against the
shutters to catch the singsong of lessons inside. He never
joined, but he devoured the sound of it. Music made him
forget hunger, if only for a while.

One night, drawn by the sound of fiddles, he lingered
near a cabaret. The tune spilled into the street, wild and
quick, a reel that made the air feel alive. For a moment,
he forgot the cold hollow in his belly, and he let the
rhythm lift him.

The door swung open. Laughter poured out with the
smoke, and a man stepped into the rain—older, silver
temples, an umbrella dangling loose in his hand. Julien
saw the gleam of silk, the carved handle catching the
lamplight. Fine work. Worth two meals. Perhaps three.

The man's mind was still on the tavern, his grip careless, attention elsewhere. The umbrella swung loose at
his side.

Julien's stomach clenched. His hands were already
cold, already empty. The music still played inside—that
wild, bright reel—and something in it made him reckless.

He darted close, seized the shaft, and tore it free.

For an instant, it was his.

He ran.

The alley swallowed him—narrow, slick with rain.
His boots slapped the stones, the umbrella clutched tight
against his ribs. Behind him, shouts erupted. Boots, heavy
and close.

He turned sharply, vaulted a crate, ducked beneath

an awning. His lungs burned. The umbrella was awkward in his grip, too long, catching on doorframes as he fled. But he held on.

Left at the baker's. Right past the pump. The Marais was a maze, but Julien knew every bolt-hole, every shadow.

The boots kept coming. He risked a glance back—

A hand like iron closed on his collar, yanking him back so hard that the breath shot from his chest. He twisted, but the grip only tightened, hauling him off his feet. He looked up and saw the red face, the bleary eyes, the uniform blotched with drink. The parrot's head was wrenched from his grasp.

Then the world slammed shut.

The blow came before he could cry out—wood cracking against bone, a white flash of pain hotter than fire. The sound split the air, louder than the fiddles, sharper than the laughter spilling from the tavern door.

Julien reeled. Blood filled his eye, warm and sticky, running down his cheek. The hand released him at last, and he crumpled to the stones. Laughter still echoed behind him, jeers ringing as though the whole quarter had seen. He scrambled to his feet, dizzy and humiliated, and stumbled into the dark.

Later, pressed into the crook of an alley, he touched his temple and felt the gash swelling, the skin torn and wet. Paris had marked him—brutal and permanent.

And yet, even through the throbbing, he found himself humming the reel he had heard at the tavern—ragged, off-key, but his.

♣ ♣ ♣

He grew sharper still in the years that followed. The market was his schoolroom, the alleys his lessons. He learned to read faces like ledgers: who would give a copper for carrying a bundle, who would look away if he lifted a crust, who would cuff him hard for coming too near.

When he was twelve, he met *Maître Marchand.* The man had an eye for boys who listened more than they spoke. Marchand promised work—carrying parcels, running notes across the quarter—and sometimes paid, though never enough. What he offered most was survival: the warmth of a tavern hearth, dregs of stew, a crust. Julien followed him as a stray dog would, wary, but unwilling to walk away.

He most clearly remembered the day when the widow came through Les Halles, the umbrella in her hands. She walked with pride, and a look of gratitude marked her features. Children frolicked at her side, voices lifted in a tune that made the air feel brighter.

Marchand's smile was already waiting. He called to her, claimed the umbrella as his. When she denied him, he beckoned the boys forward—Julien among them.

Julien saw her face—the disbelief, the sudden hollowing. Her hands trembled, stripped of more than a simple object.

Months later, the storm came. Julien had weathered storms before, pressed under eaves or curled in a doorway, but this one broke differently. The square filled with panic—voices raised, stalls collapsing. He ducked behind a cart, ready to vanish as he always did.

And then he saw it—again. The umbrella—black

silk, parrot's head gleaming—cutting through the rain, commanding the sky itself. For an instant, his stomach dropped, and the scar on his brow ached like it had been struck afresh. He had last seen it clutched by Marchand, stolen with lies—and it was now in the captain's hand.

Julien froze. Girard had cuffed him bloody in the alley. The man was to be feared. Yet here he was, stooping to gather them in, the storm breaking harmlessly over the canopy he held.

Julien's heart hammered. He could have fled—should have fled. Instead, he stepped forward. The silk stretched wider than it should have—wide enough for him. His forehead burned in the wet light as he slipped beneath it, his breath catching. He thought he smelled iron and roses.

He looked up, water streaming from his hair, and for the first time, he did not see only the officer's fists. He saw a man. He saw the canopy. He saw the impossible circle of dry stone around them, the hush of rain held back.

And he could not look away.

# LA RENCONTRE
*The Meeting*

He had meant to steal it. Not to keep, not to sell—but to return.

From the moment Marchand strutted off with the widow's umbrella, Julien had carried the thought like a stone in his chest. He had been part of that silence, a boy nodding when he should have spoken, and the shame clung to him more stubbornly than hunger.

So, when he saw it again—black silk lifted in Girard's hand during the storm—his mind leapt to the only plan he knew: wait, follow, and steal it back.

But Girard had given it to him. Placed it in his hands without force, without demand.

More remarkable still, the captain had looked him in the eye, voice low and unguarded, and said he was sorry—more or less. The brutal enforcer who had marked his forehead now turned away in regret.

Now Julien had the umbrella.

He walked—not to the markets, nor to Marchand, but to the École Communale on Rue des Martyrs. He remembered her face in Les Halles, remembered how she sang with her pupils, remembered how she had been robbed before his eyes.

He had done nothing then.

Now he crossed the yard, the parrot's head glinting dully in the sun, and waited.

When the morning bell released the pupils, Éloïse

stepped out among them. Her voice still shaped their song as they spilled into the courtyard, though time had etched a faint weariness into her grace. She stopped when she saw him—a boy thin as a shadow, scar cutting his brow, clutching *l'ouvrage* to his chest.

He stepped forward, awkward, and held it out. His voice rasped, low and broken.

"It's yours," he said hoarsely. "From Les Halles. I saw what happened." His fingers tightened on the shaft. *"Je suis désolé"*—"I'm sorry."

Her throat tightened. She reached, fingers closing around the parrot's head. In an instant, she felt the hush she had once known, the comfort that had been stripped from her in the market. It should have been anger she felt—but instead, her eyes blurred.

*"Merci,"* she whispered. Her hand brushed his for the briefest moment. "And I forgive you."

The boy blinked, startled, as though the words were foreign to him.

Éloïse glanced at the street, then back at him. "Come inside. It's warm."

He hesitated. The smell of the street clung to his clothes. Hunger warred with wariness. But when she opened the schoolhouse door and beckoned, he followed.

Inside, the little room smelled of chalk and ink, familiar to her, strange to him. She drew her basket from the desk, unwrapped her noonday bread and cheese, and tore it in half. "Here," she said, offering it. "Sit."

He sat, clutching the food as though it might vanish. He ate quickly, then slowed, watching her, unsure of her generosity. She left him in silence, letting the warmth of the room and the taste of bread do their work.

When he finished the last bite, crumbs scattered on the desk, Éloïse folded the cloth back in her basket. The quiet lingered, softer now. She studied him—the thin frame, the wary eyes, the scar like a brand across his brow.

"What's your name?" she asked quietly.

He swallowed, as though even this cost effort. "Julien."

Her lips curved faintly. "I'm Éloïse."

He nodded once, uncertain whether to meet her eyes.

"And your parents?" she asked after a pause.

Julien shrugged.

Her chest tightened. She let the silence hold before asking, "Where do you live?"

He shrugged again. "Wherever's dry."

"Do you go to school?"

Another shake of the head, sharper this time. "Too old for orphan school."

Éloïse drew a long breath. Her gaze softened.

"Do you like music, Julien?"

# LE REFUGE
*The Shelter*

The room had finished hosting children for the day. Chalk dust hung where the sun cut the air, and the little stove ticked to itself as it swallowed the last stick of wood. Éloïse set *l'ouvrage* against the door, the parrot's head watching, and laid a fresh towel across the desk as if setting a table.

"Your hands," she said.

Julien looked at them as though they belonged to someone else. Grime was ground into the lines. She poured water from the kettle into a basin, swirled in a drop of soap until the surface went opalescent, and set it before him. He glanced at the door, then at her, then lowered his fingers. When the heat reached him, he closed his eyes, and a tremor crossed his brow.

"There's warm water yet," she said softly. "Take your time."

He washed as though it were the first time. She passed him a worn cloth and turned away, granting him the privacy of her shoulders. The room smelled of soap now, and of bread that had once been warm.

"Your shirt," she said after a time. "Let me see."

He hesitated, then unbuttoned it. The fabric had lost the idea of cloth; it was more holes than shirt. She made a small sound in her throat—not disapproval, not pity, just a seamstress's assessment. From her basket, she drew a needle and a skein of thread and set to work at the desk, her fingers moving with the old ease learned at her mother's knee. He watched the needle flash and vanish, flash and vanish, as she stitched life back into the weave.

Inside the cupboard above the blackboard sat a long case, rubbed smooth by a lifetime of hands. She had carried it back from her apartment the week she returned to teaching—unable to bear its silence there, needing it near children instead of in the empty flat—then locked it away. The clasps were dark with disuse. Julien's gaze kept returning to it without meaning to. Éloïse noticed and looked away at once.

"Boots," she said, as much to herself as to him. "We'll find you a pair that know the size of your feet."

"How?" His voice was hoarse, but steadier now.

"Madame Besson keeps a trove of what boys out-grow," Éloïse said. "She never throws away a thing that might be needed."

They went down the narrow hall to the courtyard pump. The sky had paled from pewter to tin; rain hung undecided over the roofs. Madame Besson peered from her lodge, eyes sharp as bobbins. Éloïse explained in few words. The concierge listened, lips pursed, then jerked her head toward a small storeroom that smelled of var-nish and winter wool.

"A cot," she said. "Canvas. Clean enough. No talk to the headmaster. I am blind after six o'clock."

Éloïse drew out a coin.

Madame Besson pushed her hand back. "Keep it. If I take it, I may start seeing things."

"Thank you," Éloïse said.

Madame Besson sniffed, then rooted around under

a shelf. She produced a pair of scuffed boots and two pairs of thick socks. "Try."

Julien sat on the cot and pulled them on. They were too large; then, with the addition of the second pair of socks, merely generous. He stood, and the soles spoke a new sound on the floor—a sound that had a future in it.

Back in the classroom, dusk thinned the chalk lines on the board. Éloïse lit the lamp. Its glass caught the room and made it smaller, kinder.

"You may sleep in Madame Besson's storeroom tonight," she said. "Just tonight," she added, and hated the word as it left her mouth. "Tomorrow, we will think of tomorrow."

He nodded. The little cot in the storage room behind the concierge's lodge would be like a kingdom. For a moment, his face was unguarded and younger than his years.

She crossed to the cupboard and touched the long case with the backs of her fingers, as if to greet an old friend without waking him. The metal of the clasps held the cold of winters. Her hand hovered, then dropped.

"Not tonight," she said—to the case, or to herself.

On the desk lay *l'ouvrage* where she had set it, black silk furled tight, the parrot's head dull in the lamplight. She lifted it and stood with it between them. For a heartbeat, she only held it, feeling the calm she had once known.

The silk fluttered. Éloïse nodded.

*"Écoute,"* she said. *"Les règles sont simples. Pas à vendre. Pas à garder. Pour un cœur vrai."*

Then she turned the handle and set the carved beak

into his palm.

At first, it was only wood and silk. Then something in the balance changed, subtle as a key turning in a lock. The curve of the handle learned the notch of his thumb; the weight drew down and steadied not at his wrist, but along his forearm.

The lamplight narrowed and held.

His shoulders dropped, and his breath ran all the way to the bottom, the way it did under an eave when rain came sudden and hard.

Éloïse didn't move. In her hand, *l'ouvrage* had always been a comfort returning; in his, it became alert—leaning, almost, toward the door. She watched the small change in him: his stance found a center, and the wary tilt of his head eased. The scar at his brow was less like a brand and more like a seam that had been closed.

"It … fits," she said, confirming something the room already knew. "Like it knows where to be."

She touched the parrot's head gently. "It isn't to be kept, Julien—not by me, not by you. It finds who needs it most." She met his eyes. "Carry it well. Help others when you can. And when it's time, pass it on."

He lifted it an inch, testing. The silk whispered. A clean smell, iron and roses, filled the air. He swallowed, and the fear that someone would snatch it away did not vanish, but it loosened its teeth.

"But it came back to you," he protested weakly.

"For a street's length," she replied. "It has more streets in you."

His fingers closed, awkward and careful, around the

handle again. The bead of water that had lingered on the beak slid and fell, noiseless on the floorboards. The lamp flame steadied and burned a touch higher.

*L'ouvrage* was home—again.

They ate a simple supper—Lemaire's bowl from the bakery, rich and peppery—elbows almost touching at the desk. She insisted that he take the last piece of bread. After, she showed him how to fold the towel neat as a book and set a small cake of soap on it. The lamp swam in the windowpane; beyond it, the yard was an ink wash.

"At dawn," she said, "you'll come back to help me set the room before lessons. After … we will see."

He glanced at the cupboard where the long case slept. "Tomorrow?"

"Tomorrow," she said.

She blew out the lamp. In the brief darkness, she felt his presence like a bird settling its feathers. At the door, she touched his shoulder and then *l'ouvrage* in a kind of blessing.

They crossed the courtyard together. Madame Besson was already "blind," and the bolt turned in the storeroom lock, as expected. Éloïse set the towel and soap on a crate and stepped back. The cot took Julien's weight with a small canvas sigh.

He leaned the umbrella against the rough plank wall. Even in the dimness, the parrot's profile kept its watch.

"Sleep," she said. "Tomorrow, we will think of tomorrow."

He nodded. "Good night, Madame Éloïse."

"Good night, Julien."

# LE VIOLON
*The Violin*

Morning came pale and clean. Julien was already at the schoolhouse when Éloïse arrived, *l'ouvrage* under his arm, broom in his hand. Together they set the benches straight and patted chalk from the erasers until the air ghosted white.

When the bell rang, he slipped out by the side door and waited in the lee of the lodge. Lessons passed—numbers, a map of rivers, the little ones' song—and at last, the day exhaled its children back into the street.

She stood at the doorway, watching the last of them disappear into the Marais, then stepped back inside. The room held still.

She crossed to the window and beckoned. Julien appeared a moment later, shutting the door quietly behind him.

"Come," she said, and moved to the cupboard above the blackboard.

She took out the small ring of keys she wore on a ribbon and chose the one that knew the lock by heart. The clasps lifted with their old, reluctant sigh. She lifted the case down and set it on her desk, then eased back the lid. The smell rose at once—rosin and sleep and the faintest memory of winter wool.

She checked the bridge, the pegs, the dull line of strings.

"They've loosened a little," she murmured.

She wound each one toward a pitch only she could hear, stopping to draw a single testing note that hung in the room like a thread.

Julien stood close enough to see the varnish take the light and swim, hands in his pockets. *L'ouvrage* waited by the door, listening.

She rosined the bow—small, patient strokes, like waking a limb after sleep—then tucked the violin against her collarbone. A first scale came out thin; she stopped as if her hands had stepped to the edge of a remembered street and the stones were missing.

She lowered the instrument.

"Here," she said, and offered it. The bow lay across her palm, waiting.

He didn't move at first. "I don't know how."

"We'll see what you know." She stood close. "Left hand first—gently. Thumb here, opposite your first finger." She guided his hand to the neck. "Not strangling it. Light."

He gripped too hard. She touched his knuckles. "Pretend you're holding something alive—something that might fly away if you squeeze."

He loosened his grip, uncertain.

She turned his wrist with two fingers so the knuckles floated square to the fingerboard. "Good. The weight lives in your arm, not your hand." She pressed his shoulder down. "And breathe."

He nodded, still tense.

She lifted the violin and set its edge into the notch below his jaw. He jerked slightly at the unfamiliar pressure.

"Not your teeth—here," she guided, touching the spot. "Just rest it. Your head is the third hand." She adjusted the angle. "Don't clamp. Let it sit."

He held very still, as if the instrument might shatter.

"Now the bow." She took his right hand in both of hers. The wooden stick felt strange in his palm—longer than he expected, surprisingly heavy at one end. She showed him the leather grip near the base. "Hold here. Thumb bent—soft, underneath. Make a curve with it, not a hook."

She shaped his fingers: "First finger rests heavy at the knuckle. These two…" She guided his middle fingers. "… drape over like they're just visiting. And this one…" She lifted his pinky. "… stands on top to balance everything."

His hand cramped trying to remember it all.

"Don't think so hard," she said gently. "Feel it. The bow wants to move." She lifted and lowered his wrist once, showing him the motion. "The arm travels. The wrist speaks."

She stepped back.

He stared at the bow hovering above the strings, suddenly aware of how many things he was supposed to remember at once.

"Draw it across. Slowly. Straight as you can."

The first stroke said everything a first stroke says: it complained. He flinched, then huffed a small laugh at himself.

"Again," she said, touching his hand just enough to change the lane of the bow. "Closer to the bridge.

Straight—imagine you are drawing a line across a pane of glass."

He drew the bow. The second sound was less a scratch than a word with an accent. She adjusted the angle of his elbow with a fingertip; the tone smoothed, a narrow river finding its bank.

He closed his eyes.

She sang a note—*"laaaa"*—and he hunted for it without looking. When he found it, the room approved in the small way rooms do, by giving the sound a place to sit. She sang a simple classroom phrase—no more than a few steps:

*"Laaaa de la la la."*

—and he followed, crooked at first, then nearer.

She lifted the melody a step; he came with it. She shifted time, clapped a new pattern; he fitted the notes into it, untidy and then neat. They went higher until his head tipped, not because the notes required it, but because the light seemed to be there behind his closed eyes.

After a time, she stopped singing.

He played on. A thread he had found himself—slow, then surer, pausing to breathe. It wasn't any song she knew; still, something at its center was familiar. It rocked in five notes, cradled close: a low note, then a higher one, held like a bell, back to low, a quick lift above, then home again.

Soft and sure it went:

*do—sōōō—si—ré—do.*

Beautiful. Haunting.

Éloïse smiled.

She took the bow, turned his hand, and showed him a tiny circle at the frog—"the wrist warms the tone; the arm needn't shout"—then set the wood back in his fingers.

He tried. The note obeyed in part and refused in part—the honest way of good wood and new hands:

*do—sōōō—si—ré—do.*

"How do you find them without looking?" she asked.

He frowned at nothing, eyes still shut. "They're not where I look," he said. "They're where I hear."

"Good." Éloïse smiled again.

She shifted him half an inch, then a breath more. "Better. Let the first finger lead; the others will follow its courage."

They worked until his fingertips reddened and bore thin grooves where the strings had pressed. A dull ache woke in his forearm. He shook the hand out and winced.

"Enough," she said, hearing the ache. "Pain is a poor teacher. We'll stop before it begins to lie." She massaged the back of his hand once, brisk and quick, then let it go.

He lowered the instrument. He opened his eyes and blinked at the ordinary room as if it had moved while he had them closed.

Éloïse too was different now: pride alive in her eyes, resolve settling at the corners of her mouth.

"You'll need a teacher," she said. "A real one. And a place in the school that will write your name on a line." She drew a scrap from the copybook drawer and wrote as she spoke.

"First, Monsieur Fournier—at the Hôtel de Ville. He can see that there is a line to write on, even if other lines are missing. Then, Maître Valette, Rue des Trois-Frères—he can set your hand properly, give you scales and sins to confess to the metronome. If Valette agrees there is more in you than luck, we'll ask him for a letter. With that, the headmaster can place you in lessons that count, and later—if the door opens—the *Conservatoire* can be spoken of without laughter."

He touched the edge of the desk with two fingers, careful not to touch the instrument. "My name," he said, and tested how it felt to say only that.

"Yes," she said, meeting his eyes. "A name that belongs on a page and a door. Monsieur Fournier can help with the page. I will help with the door."

He didn't ask who Monsieur Fournier was, or what the *Conservatoire* meant beyond the shape of the word. He only nodded—and the stones of Paris shifted, a passage opening where none had ever been.

They ate the heel of bread left from the morning and a cut of apple she had saved for herself and forgotten. Outside, the day had decided on rain after all; it pattered softly on the yard. She drew the cloth over the violin like a light blanket, but left the case open, as if the music might need to walk in and out without asking.

"At dawn," she said, "come help me set the room before lessons. After, we'll practice. Then we'll see Monsieur Fournier."

"And tonight?" he asked, glancing toward the hall.

"Madame Besson's blindness has persisted," she said.

He smiled at that—the small, private kind that comes

with a bed of one's own, even for a night.

"Tomorrow?" he questioned.

"Tomorrow," she answered.

He went out into the soft rain. The silk opened with a sound like breath, and for a moment, the yard was two places at once—wet and not wet—and the line between them moved where he did.

Outside, the storm begins to ease. Not breaking—just pausing. Through the fogged glass, I can see the rain thinning to silver threads, the streetlamps swimming back into focus.

You feel it too—I can see it in the way you've stopped fidgeting with your glass.

Let me set this final piece where it belongs.

LA VOIX DE LA PLUIE
*"The Voice of the Rain"*
LIVRE VII

# LIVRE VII :
# LA VOIX DE LA PLUIE

## L'HÉRITAGE
*The Inheritance*

By the time the last slates were stacked and the courtyard rinsed of footsteps, the lamplighter had begun his slow constellations along Rue des Martyrs. They set out then—Éloïse with her scarf knotted twice, Julien with *l'ouvrage* under his arm. The streets shone; the Hôtel de Ville lifted its stone shoulders into lamplight.

Inside, the corridor smelled of ink and damp wool. The porter saw them, straightened, and tipped his cap. "Monsieur Fournier is in," he said excitedly.

Fournier's door stood ajar at the small office: green blotter, two chairs, a pot of violets that did not quite forgive winter. He looked up and lit up.

"Madame Éloïse! You've come." His eyes caught the umbrella and froze. "But—*l'ouvrage*… I thought—"

He stopped himself, the surprise giving way to pleasure. "May I?"

Julien offered it. Fournier weighed the handle for a heartbeat, the parrot's head bright in the lamplight. "So, it has chosen you," he said, impressed. He turned the balance once—respectful as with a badge—then placed the handle back into Julien's palm.

"Let's get started, then. We'll go gently," he said, his voice firm but soft—the tone of a man who'd learned that order and kindness need not oppose each other. He drew the register near, uncorked the ink, and let the nib wait. "Answer what you can. We'll find the rest."

His eyes settled on Julien.

"What do people call you—truly? In the markets, at the pump?"

"Julien," he said. "Sometimes 'boy.'"

"Who looks out for you? Anyone you can name."

He glanced at Éloïse. "No one, sir."

Fournier paused, then continued. "Address?"

"Care of the École Communale, Rue des Martyrs," Éloïse said. "Madame Besson is … amenable."

Fournier's mouth twitched. "Her blindness after six is a civic blessing." The nib scratched. He blew lightly to dry the stroke, then turned to a smaller book. "For the school, they will want a certificate of identity, a residence for the page, and a name they can speak aloud at roll call. Where have you lived—before Madame Besson's?"

Julien's fingers found the chair's edge and held it. "At the Hospice des Enfants-Trouvés—years. Dormitory windows, long rows of bunks. After … sometimes a workroom, sometimes the street."

"Were you left at *la roue*?" Fournier asked—gentle, direct.

"So the sisters said," Julien answered.

"And your given name—Julien—from the calendar? A saint's day?"

He nodded. "They said so."

Fournier set down the pen, rose, and crossed to a tall cabinet. "One moment."

There was nothing bureaucratic in it; he was pleased, intent.

The hinges gave a sigh as he opened the door, revealing shelves close-packed with ledgers in every shade of brown. He stood a moment, reading the spines as one might read the years of his own life, then drew one free—hesitated—and took another to join it. He carried both to the desk, set them side by side, and began with the older.

Pages went by like streets, slow and familiar, each marked by a name, a date, a note in the margin. From time to time, his finger paused, hovered, moved on.

Something there caught, but not enough; he closed the book gently, replaced it with the second, and opened again farther in. The paper thinned, the ink grew more delicate, the handwriting older, tighter. He turned a few pages, then rose once more, crossing back to the press to fetch a third—thicker, bound in cracked green leather.

At last, his face changed. He laid a marker across the gutter and bent close over a narrow column whose ink had dried to the color of old violets.

"Here! Here you are."

He turned the book so they could see.

The line was clean, the hand compact and true.

### Julien Pluvier

*orphelin, sans demeure;*

*note: hospice (jour de St-Julien).*

Julien didn't speak. He stared at the letters as if a door had decided, at last, to be a door.

The room held its breath. His name—his own name—sat there in ink, shaped by a hand that had never known him, yet had left a space waiting all the same.

Something in his chest lifted as though a life he had only borrowed were now being given back.

"Good," Fournier said, already moving. He filled in the date, added, *Résidence: École Communale, Rue des Martyrs (provisoire),* and cross-referenced the school ledger. He drew the red wax close, warmed it, pressed in the Hôtel de Ville seal, and signed his name with the calm of a man responsible for what he has done.

He sat, drawing out a clean sheet. *"Extrait du registre d'identité,"* he said, half to the page, half to the room. The nib spoke its small thunder. He copied the essentials, sanded the line, tipped the page until the grains whispered off, and stamped the seal once more.

He slid the paper across the blotter, and when Julien looked up, Fournier was smiling.

"Monsieur Pluvier, you exist."

Julien did not reach at once. He looked at the *extrait* as he had looked at the violin, unsure where its weight wanted to be.

Fournier folded it once, twice, wrapped it in oiled cloth, tied the string.

"A parcel," he said. "Easier to believe than a miracle."

He added two more pages—*Attestation pour inscription scolaire* and a brief note to Maître Valette, Rue des Trois-Frères:

*Le porteur a un nom, un lieu pour se tenir. Aider, ne pas refuser*—"The bearer has a name, a place to stand. Help, do not turn him away.”

He pushed the small stack to Julien. “Keep these dry.” His eyes went again to *l'ouvrage*, now with open affection. “I see you're equipped.”

Éloïse found her breath and a smile. “Thank you.”

“Indulge me,” Fournier said, already rising. “My coach is at the east door. It will take you home. Tonight deserves a ride.”

They did not argue.

At the east door, the coach waited with lamps like small moons. Rain stitched the square into glossy cloth.

“Home,” Fournier told the driver. “The school on Rue des Martyrs.”

Julien tucked the parcel inside his shirt and opened *l'ouvrage* as they crossed to the step. He held it aloft, and it settled there, sheltering them both, the rain whispering approval against its skin.

Éloïse settled into the coach first; Julien followed. As the coach departed, Fournier lifted a hand from the doorway—a gesture that said both *“Good night”* and *“I will answer for you if required.”*

Under the coach's small roof, the city moved by in damp light. The seal on the parcel warmed against Julien's chest. He looked down once, then out at the rain.

“Monsieur Pluvier,” Éloïse tried, tasting the full weight of it.

Julien nodded. “It sits well,” he said.

The coach turned toward Rue des Martyrs.

Somewhere, a bell struck the hour and held a breath between tones, remembering a five-note cradle that belonged to the rain.

# LE MAÎTRE
*The Master*

Morning brought a cleaner cold. The coach had left them at the schoolhouse door the night before. Now the street was quiet—only boots and breath in the early light.

Rue des Trois-Frères woke in shutters and brooms. They found the number set back from the pavement, a bell-pull shiny where hands had hoped.

A narrow staircase rose to a room with two windows and a stove. On one wall: a metronome, a clock, a map of scales pinned in a sun-faded grid. On the other: an instrument stand like a small forest, cases stacked like patient coffers. A cat assessed them and chose indifference.

*"Entrez,"* said a voice that had spent its life teaching wood to listen.

Maître Valette was narrow as a violin bow, white at the temples, his cuffs shiny where sleeves met desks. He took them in without hurry—the woman with a teacher's posture, the boy too thin for his boots, the umbrella he knew by reputation (though he pretended not to), and the violin case that made something flicker behind his eyes.

Éloïse offered the paper from Fournier. Valette read without sitting:

*Extrait du registre d'identité—Julien Pluvier.*

*Le porteur a un nom, un lieu pour se tenir. Aider, ne pas refuser.*

He looked up. "Monsieur Pluvier," he said, "welcome."

Julien blinked at the name on someone else's tongue and nodded.

Valette tapped the metronome lightly, not to start it, but to wake the idea of time. "We won't waste yours. Show me your hands."

Julien held them out. The fingertips bore the faint grooves of yesterday's strings.

"Good," Valette said. "They've begun to argue with you."

He set a chair and the stand to their small heights. "Madame," he said to Éloïse, and his eyes softened a fraction at the case. "May I?"

She set it on the table. He opened it with a mechanic's attention and a friend's quiet. "This wood knows grief," he murmured, not unkindly. "It needs to weep."

He checked the bridge, sighted the fingerboard, tested the pegs, turned the strings up toward pitches the room recognized without effort. Then he rosined the bow carefully.

"Sit," he told Julien. "We start at the beginning—and also at the end."

Left hand: he turned the wrist the breath it needed, lifted a collapsing knuckle with one fingertip. Right hand: thumb round and soft, first finger's weight honest, the little finger ready on top. "The arm travels," he said. "The wrist speaks. The finger listens to both."

He placed the bow to the string. "Open strings only. Four long bows. Don't hurry."

Julien drew the bow. The first note trembled into

being, then found its shape. The next came easier, and the third knew where it belonged. Something was taking form—not music yet, but the promise of it.

Valette nodded once. "Again. Close your—" He stopped himself when he saw Julien's eyes already closed.

He moved quickly and exactly: whole bows, then halves; near the bridge, then away; a little circle at the frog to warm the note without making it larger. He clapped a rhythm; the boy fit breath into it and then sound. When the hand tired, he switched to ear.

"Listen." He sang *laaa* and a second tone above; he did not say their names. "Find me this, then that."

The boy hunted without looking and arrived not by the eye, but by a path that only he knew.

Valette changed the interval without warning; the boy followed late, then less late, then on time.

"What have you been taught?" Valette asked.

"Nothing," Julien said.

Valette went very still. He studied the boy's face for the telltale vanity of that word and found none—only the truth, delivered plainly.

For a long moment, the master said nothing. His eyes moved from Julien's callused fingertips to the violin, then back again. When he finally spoke, his voice was quieter, more careful.

"You've been taught by nothing," he said slowly. He set the bow down with deliberate gentleness, as though suddenly aware that he was handling something fragile. "What you have—" He paused, choosing his words. "Most students I see for years never find what you found in minutes."

Éloïse's breath caught.

Valette turned to her, his expression unreadable. "Madame, you've brought me a gift I don't deserve." He looked back at Julien. "And a great deal of work."

He turned to the instrument cases along the wall, hands clasped behind his back. "We will not waste this," he said, almost to himself. Then, louder: "First position only, no heroics. Scales will be your bread. We will not play music; we will build the mouth that can speak it."

He turned to Julien. "You will hate me at intervals," he said, almost apologizing, "but less as we continue."

Valette set an easy phrase on the stand, no more than five notes that turned and came home. "Read that. No shame in singing first."

Julien sang under his breath, testing the floor. He did not know he was singing anything at all. When he put bow to string, his first retelling was crooked; the second held. On the third, a color entered the tone that was not yet music and not yet absent.

Valette's head tilted, listening not to the accuracy, but to the way the boy changed direction without being told which way was north.

"Again," he said.

They worked until the wrist said stop. Valette watched for it exactly.

"Enough." He put the violin on the table and covered it with a cloth as one covers a sleeping child.

"Terms," he said, returning to the blotter. "One lesson each week here. Practice daily at the school before bells—two pages, no arguments. Madame will supervise and correct, and I will correct her correcting. When the hand matches the ear, we will talk about pieces. When both match the heart, we will stop talking."

Éloïse inclined her head. "Agreed."

Julien spoke quietly from the corner. "I have no money, sir. I cannot pay you."

"Money." Valette laughed. "You will ignore it." He saw Julien ready to protest. "Paris has asked me to help, and I am arrogant enough to do as I am asked."

He wrote a small note for the headmaster with his own name and a half-dozen uncompromising words. He slid it across with a pencil stub and a small cloth-bound copy of scales whose corners had learned humility. "This you keep. Do not lend it; I want the grease from your fingers to darken the corners as proof."

Julien took the book as if it might reject him. It did not.

Valette stood. "Next week, same hour. Bring the instrument; I will reset the soundpost once you've bullied the top into remembering that it should resonate."

At the door, he paused. "Monsieur Pluvier."

Julien looked up.

"You have a way of finding notes that aren't where eyes put them," Valette said. "That is dangerous—and precious. We will teach your hands to deserve your ears."

On the stairs, the cat escorted them to the second turn and then lost interest. Outside, the street's narrow light received them. It had begun to rain again, a polite rain with no opinion of its own.

Julien opened *l'ouvrage*. The silk found its curve again, and the parrot's head faced the hill.

"Homework," Éloïse said, half dread, half delight.

"Two pages," Julien replied, beaming.

# L'INSCRIPTION
*The Registration*

Late morning brought a stubborn light to Rue des Martyrs. The children were at sums; the yard was rinsed and quiet. Éloïse crossed with Julien to the headmaster's door.

The office kept a coal fire that sighed and made the ledgers steam at their edges. The desk was old enough to be courteous, and the chair behind it had learned when to creak. On the wall hung a faded map of the *arrondissements* and a clock that clicked like patient shoes.

The headmaster looked up—a solid man, tidy mustache, ink at the nail of his thumb.

"Madame Éloïse," he said. "And you must be Julien." He looked at the boy, assessing. "Papers?"

Éloïse laid them out: *Extrait du registre d'identité*—Julien Pluvier, the red seal pressed proud; and beneath it, the note in Monsieur Fournier's clean, uncompromising hand:

*Le porteur a un nom, un lieu pour se tenir. Aider, ne pas refuser.*

The headmaster read once, then again, then checked the seal as a man greets an old colleague. "Fournier," he said, the way some men say "rain." He set the papers square and met the boy's eyes.

"Julien Pluvier," he tried, and found the name fit the room. "Sit."

He asked as a man who has asked many times and

wishes to do it properly.

"Where have you slept?"

Julien hesitated. "The street, mostly. Last night—"
He glanced at Éloïse.

"Last night he stayed in the storage room," Éloïse
said carefully. "With Madame Besson's permission. She
said nothing official, of course."

The headmaster's eyebrows rose slightly. He set down
his pen. "Madame Besson is remarkably blind after six
o'clock," he said, his tone giving nothing away. "Professionally so."

A long pause.

"Can you rise early without becoming useless by
noon? We are not a monastery."

"Yes," he said.

"What work do you know? Brooms, pails, coal, wood,
errands?"

"Yes," he said again. "And sums."

That made the headmaster's mouth think about a
smile. "Sums will be tested. As for letters—"

"Uneven," Éloïse said, not apologizing. "We have
begun."

The headmaster tapped the edge of the *extrait*. "Paris
recognizes you. That eases our conscience and sharpens
our obligations." He opened the daybook and dipped
the pen. "We can admit you for one month. Trial. Con-
ditions: punctuality, attendance, conduct. You will keep
the yard honest and the benches obedient. Morning
duties before the first bell—coal, water, sweeping. After
lessons, one hour of letters with Madame Éloïse. Each

dawn, practice—two pages, no complaints. Weekly with Maître Valette."

He looked up. "At eight, you sit in class. Not at the door, not on the stairs. In the room."

Julien nodded.

"For lodging," the headmaster went on, "the storage room cot is authorized. Not a favor. You will make payment in chores. Madame Besson will pretend not to know, and will in fact know everything. Do not put buckets where she can trip over them."

"Blind after six," Éloïse said.

"Professionally," the headmaster agreed.

He rose without ceremony and crossed to a cupboard that had outlived two regimes. From it he fetched a small slate, a stub of chalk, a folded notice, and a column of figures clipped from an old account.

"Test," he said, but gently, as one might say *"taste."* "Copy these two lines. Read this aloud to me. Add that column."

Julien set the slate on his knee. His letters came in fits—an easy *J* that liked to be admired, a stubborn *u* that did not. The lines made it to the margins, but not in parade. He read the notice haltingly, spine straight, the words arriving like boys late to class.

At the figures, he stopped being careful and simply was. The hand ran calm, carried properly, came home on the last digit without ceremony.

The headmaster watched what needed watching and not a jot more. In the margin of the daybook, he wrote, small and exact: *bonne volonté; main inégale; chiffres sûrs*—"good will; uneven hand; sure figures."

He closed the book as if that settled it, because it did.

"Welcome, Monsieur Pluvier," he said, and shook the boy's hand as he would shake a father's. "You are a student of this school now. The rules apply to you because you are one of us."

Julien beamed.

The headmaster looked at the umbrella then, as one looks at weather that has insisted on attending a meeting. "Hooks are by the lodge door," he said. "Use the second from the left. It drips least on the slate pile. If you disobey gravity in the corridors, Madame Besson will declare a flood, and I shall be forced to agree with her."

"Second from the left," Julien repeated.

The headmaster stacked the papers with an efficiency that did not insult their importance. "If anyone questions the *extrait*," he added, "they may question me. Monsieur Fournier is not the only person who signs his name on purpose."

He rose; the chair creaked just the right amount. "That is all. Be early tomorrow. Today—go learn where the buckets live and where they do not. Then eat."

Back at the lodge, Julien set the parcel on the stool in his room and untied Fournier's knot. The *extrait* lay on top, the seal a small red circle. Beneath it, the note from Valette; beneath that, the little book of scales whose corners would one day turn dark.

He put his hand on the bed, greeting it. He set the papers under the pillow. The clock in the corridor ticked the school's heartbeat. Somewhere above, a mop was shushed. Rain found the tiles and began a quiet argument with them.

Julien lay back and watched the slant of the window. His mouth shaped the letters once, twice:

**"Julien Pluvier."**

Under his breath, so only the room could hear, he hummed the small five-note promise that belonged to the rain:

*do—sōōō—si—ré—do.*

The rain drummed its agreement.

The day, at last, retired.

⚜ ⚜ ⚜

# L'EXAMEN

*The Test*

Four weeks braided themselves into habit. Dawn was scales and chalk dust; noon was obedient benches and pails that did not argue; dusk was letters with Éloïse. On Thursdays, Valette reset what the week had bent and gave him two more pages to quarrel with.

Madame Besson's blindness after six held, and the second hook from the left learned to drip where it should and nowhere else.

Sometime in the second week, Fournier replaced the provisional seal; the red wax cooled like a small sun on the *extrait* that lived under Julien's pillow.

The summons came on a day that smelled of flowers and cinnamon. The headmaster asked for him at the small room off the office—the one with the good clock and the quiet piano. Éloïse crossed with Julien toward the headmaster's door, the violin case in her hands, *l'ouvrage* folded beneath Julien's arm.

She stopped at the threshold and bent close.

"Breathe," she said.

Julien nodded.

Three men waited.

The headmaster stood by the window—hands clasped behind his back. Beside the desk sat Monsieur Fournier, papers stacked before him, his expression calm but watchful.

And in the chair nearest the fire sat a third man Julien did not know: narrow shoulders, silver spectacles, a coat too fine for this neighborhood. His fingers drummed once on the armrest, then stopped. Everything about him suggested a man whose time was measured and whose patience was not.

The headmaster spoke first. "Madame Éloïse. Julien. Welcome." He gestured to the stranger. "This is Monsieur Leblanc, from the *Conservatoire*. He has come at Monsieur Fournier's request."

Leblanc inclined his head—polite, but cool. "The Conservatoire scholarship committee requires direct assessment," he said. His voice carried the flatness of a man who had seen many hopeful cases and few worthy ones. "Monsieur Fournier speaks highly of you. We shall see."

Julien's throat tightened.

Fournier met his eyes and nodded once—steady, encouraging.

"Sit," the headmaster said gently, and set a chair for him.

The headmaster began with reading. He opened a worn primer and set it on the desk. "Aloud, if you please. From here."

Julien leaned forward. The letters swam, then settled. His voice came thin at first, each word a small negotiation between eye and tongue.

*"Le ... garçon ... marche ... dans ... la rue."*

The words were careful, uneven—but they arrived.

"Good," the headmaster said. "Continue."

By the third line, the rhythm found him. The stumbles lessened. When he finished, Leblanc's expression had not changed, but he made a small note in his ledger.

Next came writing. A slate, a stub of chalk. The headmaster dictated slowly: "*Paris reconnaît ses enfants.*"

Julien bent over the slate. His hand formed the letters with effort—the *P* too proud, the *s* uncertain—but the sentence took shape, legible if not elegant.

Leblanc leaned forward to inspect it. "Functional," he murmured.

Then came sums. The headmaster laid a column of figures before him—additions, a subtraction, a small multiplication tucked at the bottom like a test within a test.

Julien's hand steadied. Here the world made sense. The chalk moved surely, carried without hesitation, came home on the last digit clean and true.

He set the slate down.

Fournier smiled faintly. The headmaster's eyebrows rose. Even Leblanc paused, then wrote a longer note.

"Well," Leblanc said. "Your mind is not idle."

Julien exhaled.

"But intelligence," Leblanc continued, "is not artistry. Let us see what Maître Valette believes he has found."

Éloïse set the violin case on the desk. The clasps lifted with their old, reluctant sigh. She took out the instrument, checked the bridge, the pegs, drawing a testing note that hung in the room like a thread of smoke. She rosined the bow—small, patient strokes—then held both out to Julien. His hands trembled as he took them.

Leblanc produced a single page from his satchel and

set it on the music stand. "An étude," he said. "First position. Nothing excessive. Play it through."

Julien tucked the violin to his collarbone. His left hand found the neck; his right gripped the bow too tightly. He could feel all their eyes on him—Éloïse's confident, Leblanc's skeptical, Fournier's hopeful, the headmaster's kind.

He drew the bow.

The sound that emerged was thin, uncertain—a scratch more than a note. His fingers stumbled on the shift, and the rhythm lurched. He tried to recover, but his breath had gone shallow, his wrist locked.

He stopped halfway through, cheeks burning.

Leblanc sighed—a small sound, but it filled the room. He glanced at his pocket watch.

"Monsieur Fournier," he said quietly, "I understand your intentions, but the *Conservatoire* cannot—"

"Perhaps," Fournier interrupted, his voice firm, "Monsieur Pluvier might take a breath and begin again."

Silence.

Julien looked at Éloïse. She met his eyes and touched her own chest once, slowly—breathe.

He lowered the violin. Drew air. Let it out. The fire crackled. The clock ticked. *L'ouvrage* hung from a hook in the corner, the parrot's head watching.

He lifted the violin again. This time, he closed his eyes.

The first note came clean—not perfect, but true. The second followed, and the third found its place. His bow arm loosened; his left hand remembered what Éloïse and

Valette had taught him. The étude unfolded—modest, honest, each phrase shaped with care.

When he reached the shift, his hand moved without thinking, the muscle remembering what the mind had not yet named.

By the final measure, something deeper had emerged. Not brilliance, but sincerity. Not artistry yet, but the ground from which it might grow.

He finished and opened his eyes.

The room had gone still.

Leblanc set down his pen. "Better," he said, but it was not quite a concession. "Competent. With years of training—"

He did not finish. A sound from the corner interrupted him. *L'ouvrage* had fallen from its hook, clattering to the floor.

Julien looked toward *l'ouvrage*—then at Éloïse.

He did not hand back the violin.

Instead, he adjusted his grip slightly, settled the instrument more deeply into the curve of his jaw, and without being asked, without waiting for permission, he closed his eyes again and began to play.

Five notes. Cradled close.

A low note, then a higher one—held like a bell—back to low, a quick lift above, then home again. Soft and sure, it went:

*do—sōōō—si—ré—do.*

But now it was not just five notes. Now it opened.

His bow moved with a sureness that had not been there before, drawing the phrase out, letting it breathe.

He played it once simply, as it had been given. Then again, with a small variation—a grace note that bloomed and faded like a drop of water catching light. Then a third time, lower, darker, the melody descending into a minor shadow before climbing back into itself.

The room held its breath.

He was not performing. He was *speaking*—through wood and horsehair and gut, through the small movements of his wrist and the pressure of his fingers, through something that lived beneath technique and rose through it like a spring through a mountain.

The lullaby grew. It ached. It consoled. It remembered. It spoke of rain and sunshine. Famine and feast. Love and loss.

When at last the final note dissolved into silence, no one moved.

Éloïse's hand was pressed to her mouth. Fournier sat very still, his eyes bright. The headmaster had turned from the window, and his face bore the expression of a man who has just witnessed something he cannot name and will not forget.

Leblanc stared at Julien as though seeing him for the first time.

"Where," he said, his voice barely above a whisper, "did you learn that?"

Julien lowered the violin slowly. "I didn't learn it, *monsieur*. It was … given to me."

Leblanc rose. He crossed to Julien and bent slightly, studying his face as one might study a manuscript whose provenance is uncertain, but whose value is undeniable.

"Young man," he said quietly, "the *Conservatoire* maintains a scholarship for exceptional cases. It requires recommendation from two masters and a municipal sponsor." He glanced at Valette, then at Fournier. "It appears you have two of the three."

He straightened.

"I will add my name."

Fournier exhaled, and the sound was relief and triumph both. Outside, the bells of Saint-Paul began their slow count of the hour. The fire crackled.

The headmaster stepped forward and placed a hand on Julien's shoulder. "Monsieur Pluvier," he said, and his voice was warm, "you are a student of this school. But I suspect you will not remain here long."

Leblanc returned to his chair and wrote a final note in his ledger—longer than the others, deliberate and careful. When he finished, he closed the book with a soft thump that sounded, in that small room, like a door opening.

"The examination is complete," he said. He looked at Julien. "We will expect you at the Conservatoire when your hands are ready. Maître Valette will know when that is."

He gathered his papers, nodded to Fournier and the headmaster, and left without ceremony.

When the door closed behind him, the room exhaled.

Éloïse took the violin gently from Julien's hands and set it back in its case. His fingers were trembling. She folded them in her own.

"*Magnifique*," she whispered.

Fournier stood and crossed to Julien. He offered his

hand, and Julien took it.

"Paris recognizes you, Julien Pluvier," Fournier said. "Do not forget what that means."

The headmaster opened his daybook and wrote one line in the margin, his script small and exact: *don exceptionnel*—"exceptional gift."

He signed the enrollment card, blotted it carefully, and slid it across the desk. Julien took it with both hands.

*"Bienvenue,"* the headmaster said.

In the corner, *l'ouvrage* lay where it had fallen, the parrot's eyes bright as embers, watching. Julien bent and lifted it. The shaft was warm in his hands.

Outside, the sun was shining.

# LA MUSIQUE DU MONDE
*The Music of the World*

The city taught him by rooms. First a corner where fresh bread steam met rain; then a salon with a chandelier; then a parish hall that smelled of varnish and hope; then the *Conservatoire's* foyer, where shoes clicked like metronomes; and later—much later—a stage that made him larger than himself.

In the beginning, he played where people did not plan to listen, and found that they listened anyway. A market morning, a doorway, Éloïse at his shoulder, Valette's notes in his pocket like commands written small. He set the bow, and the lane straightened under him. Coins were tossed into his hat, not because he asked, but because a few bars made the world nicer.

The salon gave him a carpet that swallowed footsteps and a maid who had learned to make doors inaudible. He stood under lamplight that tried too hard, and bowed because others did. People called him "Monsieur Pluvier." He played an *andante* that Valette approved, and a private lullaby that belonged to no one and to everyone.

At the parish hall, he learned the swell of people. The first rows listened forward; the back rows straightened in their seats. Julien made a scale into a prayer. Valette stood near the door, bowed his head, and did not clap—which was how he clapped. After, a baker with flour under his nails shook Julien's hand and said, "I didn't know a note could taste like fresh bread."

Over time, the rooms changed countries. Trains and

borders stitched themselves behind him: a quay where gulls heckled the boats in Marseille; a silk hall in Lyon that smelled faintly of soap; a parish *fête* in Liège where coal dust clung to the applause; a Vienna salon with mirrors that multiplied courage; a Barcelona courtyard where drying sheets flapped in rhythm like billowing sails; a Swiss town that loaned him its echo.

He played in hospital wards and barracks, in orphanages, foyers, kitchens, and halls. People came on purpose or by accident, and left better for it. A measure loosened a fist, an old quarrel was finally laid to rest, a restless child slept, a grieving widow ate, a letter was finally written. Julien did not transform lives - he loosened knots, one room at a time, and carried the warmth of each room with him after.

*L'ouvrage* went everywhere with him. Porters carried it as carefully as if it were a royal scepter. Customs men lifted their eyebrows and then their hands and waved him through. Under its cover, programs stayed legible, strings stayed dry, strangers stepped in close enough to be neighbors for a spell. He learned to tilt the silk so a child's shoes found the ridges in the street and avoided the rivers between them. People who would not meet a violin's gaze would step under an umbrella's invitation, and for a breath, feel better.

More than once, he thought he had found the one meant to receive it next. A student with cracked shoes whose bow hand trembled with hunger; a mother carrying her child through the rain; a porter who whistled while shouldering the weight of other men's burdens. Each time, he felt the stirring—that faint quickening in the silk, the sense that the moment had arrived. He would raise *l'ouvrage* between them, meaning to give it freely, but something small would intervene: the student turned, called away by laughter; the mother's child cried, and she hurried on; the porter vanished through a door before he could speak.

Once, he actually offered it—both hands extended—and the woman only smiled, misunderstanding, and covered his hands with hers to keep them from the cold.

Each time, *l'ouvrage* remained—not through his will, but its own. The silk would tighten, the parrot's head turn subtly toward him, a weight in the handle reminding him: *not yet.* So, he carried it still—not as a possession, but as a promise—ready for the day it would finally refuse to stay.

In all those years, he wrote only one piece of his own—though "wrote" was not quite the word for it. The melody had always been there, carried through hunger and cold like a secret kept in the bones.

It rocked in five notes, cradled close: a low note, then a higher one, held like a bell, back to low, a quick lift above, then home again. Soft and sure it went:

*do—sōōō—si—ré—do.*

The notes came again the next night, and the night after that. He tried to chase them away, but they returned like breath, shaping every exercise until he stopped pretending they were an accident. He wrote them down in the margins of his lesson book, at first as shorthand, then as a theme.

A cradle-rock turned outward. A rain pattern turned inward.

*do—sōōō—si—ré—do.*

He called it *"Berceuse de la Pluie"*—"Lullaby of the

Rain."

Others called it *"La Musique du Monde"*—"The Music of the World."

He never told anyone that the melody felt remembered—as though someone, long ago, had hummed it to him before sleep, and the world had only been waiting for him to hum it back.

When he played it, no hall was foreign. The music carried its own translation—a language the heart already knew. Listeners with wet eyes said the tune reminded them of a window left open to the rain, or a promise they had nearly kept.

He said nothing.

A night came when the larger stage held still for him. The hall's breath gathered and waited. He lifted the bow and began *"La Musique du Monde"*—the cradle grown vast, the lullaby now dressed for company.

In the slow middle, he closed his eyes and found a note that wasn't where it was supposed to be. The sound remembered rain and hope and loss and joy—and made the room remember with it.

For a moment, he could see her—not clearly, just a shape bending over an infant, the shadow of a smile, the rhythm of a heart keeping time with the melody.

When he lowered the bow, silence filled the hall.

And then the applause was like thunder.

After, the city let him be small again. He crossed
to a café near the theater, shaking the silk once at the
threshold and keeping it with him—by his chair, not on
a hook—the parrot's eye catching a lamp and making a
little sun of it.

There was a table by the window, and a stranger who
knew how to make room. He set *l'ouvrage* where it could
rest against his coat. A waiter brought soup without being
asked, and he warmed his hands on the bowl.

He hummed, very low:

*do—sōō—do—ré—do.*

And when the room grew quiet enough to deserve
it, he began to speak.

LE PASSAGE
"The Passage"
LIVRE VIII

# LIVRE VIII :
# LE PASSAGE

Outside, the storm is doing its patient work, rinsing the city to its bones. The café windows breathe in and out, fogging and clearing, fogging and clearing. Coats steam on their hooks, cups click in their saucers, and lamplight pools on the little tables like melted gold.

"People like to call her the City of Light," I say, nodding toward the glass. "And they are not wrong. But it is in the rain that she tells us the most."

I have been speaking for some time. You are still listening. That is rarer than you think.

And before I began, I watched you. Watched you buy soup for the man whose hands shook. Watched you, outside, press your coat into the arms of someone who needed it more. You are cold now—you hide it well, but the cup in your hands tells the truth. You think these are small things.

They are not.

Paris notices such things, especially on nights like this.

"I have told you how it began," I say. "The crooked shop. The stranger. The rules. I have told you of the clerk and the widow, of a policeman who mistook cruelty for strength, of a boy who ran too fast and not fast enough." I smiled. "It is a habit of boys."

You smile too—the kind that hides more than it shows. The lamp above our table hums. For a moment, the flame leans and steadies, and in that brief lean, the light glances across my brow. You look, as anyone would, then look away the way kind people do, leaving a man his dignity. Still, you saw it—the thin, pale seam just where the hairline breaks, a forgotten punctuation mark set by a careless night and a heavy hand. I did not touch it. One does not press an old bruise to prove it still exists.

"Perhaps you think I've told you about these lives to pass the time while the sky does what it must," I go on. "It is true enough: storms like company. But that is not the whole of it."

I let the silence settle between us the way a craftsman lets lacquer cure. It is a poor thing, a story rushed.

At my feet, something shifts against the table leg with a soft note—wood on wood, the barest tap. You glance down, because the body knows before the mind. A handle, carved into the head of a parrot, gleams where my coat has failed to hide it. Silk—folded tight, dark as midnight ink—rests against the chair. The parrot's eye catches the lamp and makes a small sun of it. Or perhaps the lamp borrowed its light back.

The waiter comes with the bill—thumb on the edge, a coin already trapped. I set down more coins than are needed and wave him on. He goes. He is a good man who pretends not to be. Paris is full of such people.

"Do you remember the rules?" I ask.

The storm makes an answer against the glass, a drum-roll you can feel in your teeth.

*"Pas à vendre. Pas à garder. Pour un cœur vrai."*

I nod. Words are a kind of weather; some arrive only once the pressure drops.

"There were years," I say, "when I imagined keeping it. I tell you that so you will not think yourself wicked if you imagine the same. We are all scoundrels, secretly. We dust our treasures, ask the price and lower it, raise it, lower it again. But this is not an object for a shelf."

I tap the table with one finger; the wood answers like a muted string.

"It is a door. It opens, and people find themselves."

Outside, the thunder retreats one block farther away. Someone laughs at the bar—the kind of laugh that breaks and heals in the same breath. The smell of fresh bread reaches us from the kitchen.

"You have storms," I say. "Some follow you, some wait ahead. They are not punishment, but memory. They are written into you—weather the soul remembers."

You do not answer—not with words. Your hand closes and opens on the edge of the table. It is surprising how much a palm can confess.

I lean down and free the parrot-headed handle from the shadow of my coat. It comes willingly, as it does when it has decided. My fingers, old creeks mapped into them, travel the familiar grain. I let the weight of it rest between us, a small length of silk and wood bridging the distance from my life to yours.

The many scents of the room are replaced by iron and roses. The lamp breathes, and the seam on my brow remembers itself.

You look at me then in the way people look at the river when they have been away too long. It is not awe.

It is relief that the water goes on.

"You are its *gardien* now," I said, and draw my hand away, leaving it where grace prefers to meet the willing.

The parrot's eye holds the lamp steady. Somewhere in the rafters, the rain finds a new path and then another, patient as a craftsman.

"When you leave," I say, "do not look for signs. *L'ouvrage* is not a fortune teller. If the wind feels wrong, change streets. If a stranger weeps, be the wall that lets them lean. If you come to a door, and the person on the other side does not know how to open it, be the hinge. That is all the magic there is."

You smile at that, though your eyes are wet. It is a common side effect of storms.

"Remember," I say, and lay the rules once more where they belong—not as words to recite, but as choices to make.

*"Pas à vendre. Pas à garder. Pour un cœur vrai"*—"Not to be sold. Not to be kept. For a true heart."

I pause, and because I am old, I allow myself one more line:

"And if ever you doubt, listen for the city in the rain. She will tell you who you are."

I stand, my knees complaining. I set my hat on my head and gather nothing else; there is nothing else to gather. The chair makes a sound like a held breath released. The parrot taps the table once and then is still.

The bell over the door lifts its voice. The night greets me with a soft hand. Outside, the storm has gentled. Rain stitches the air with a finer thread. The cobblestones shine like the backs of sleeping fish. Somewhere, very near, someone begins to play a violin under an awning, the notes bright and thin as wire, and the city's great, dark body answers with a low, contented hum:

do—sōōō—si—ré—do.

I do not look back. That is another rule, unwritten but true: when a door closes properly, you let it.

Behind me, I imagine, there is the scrape of a chair and the sound a silk canopy makes when it opens only a little—like a quiet breath before a promise. And in that small shelter, a life stands up—not new, exactly, but more itself than in the hour before.

Paris did what she always does. She took the rain and made a mirror of it, so we could see ourselves—*and not be afraid.*

**Fin.**

# ÉPILOGUE

## LE FORGERON DE LA PLUIE

*The Blacksmith of Rain*

In a corner of Paris that no map recalls, the crooked shop still leans into the street. Its shutters still sag, its paint still peels, and ivy still climbs its walls like green lace.

Inside, lamplight glows as it always has—warm as a hearth, true as a vow.

At the bench sits Guillaume De Saint-Aubin. His hair is silvered now, his hands nicked and sure. Brass ribs rest in jars; silk waits folded in midnight hues. Outside, the storm presses against the shutters like an eager customer. Guillaume bends his head, needle moving with the patience of rain.

Now and again, he pauses—lifting some imagined handle, a parrot's gaze caught in wood and stone. His eyes narrow, as though listening for words delivered long ago:

*"Pas à vendre. Pas à garder. Pour un cœur vrai."*

So, if one night, the rain finds you alone, and you wander farther than you meant to, and a crooked little shop leans into the street—step inside. You may find him there—the Blacksmith of Rain.

And you may leave with more than shelter from the storm.

⚜ ⚜ ⚜

# ANNEXE
## GLOSSAIRE DES LIEUX
*Locations*

| French | Pronunciation |
| --- | --- |
| École Communale | ay-KOHL koh-myoo-NAL |
| Les Halles | lay-AHL |
| Hospice des Enfants-Trouvés | OSS-pees dayz ahn-FAHN troo-VAY |
| Hôtel de Ville | oh-TEL duh VEEL |
| Marais | mah-RAY |
| Montmartre | mohn-MAR-truh |
| Paris | pah-REE |
| Place Pigalle | plahs pee-GAHL |
| Rue des Martyrs | roo day mar-TEER |
| Rue Saint-Antoine | roo san-tahn-TWAHN |
| Saint-Paul / Saint-Paul–Saint-Louis | san-PAWL / san-PAWL san-loo-EE |

# GLOSSAIRE DES PERSONNAGES

*Principaux Personnages - Main Characters*

| French | Pronunciation |
| --- | --- |
| Guillaume De Saint-Aubin | gee-YOHM duh san-oh-BAN |
| L'Étranger | lay-trahn-ZHAY |
| Henri Fournier | ahn-REE for-NYAY |
| Éloïse Aubert | ay-loh-EEZ oh-BEHR |
| Le Marchand | luh mar-SHAHN |
| Julien Pluvier | zhoo-LYAHN |
| Capitaine Girard | kah-pee-TEN zhee-RAHR |

# GLOSSAIRE DES TERMES ET EXPRESSIONS

*Terms and Expressions*

| French | Pronunciation |
| --- | --- |
| "À la Claire Fontaine" | "At the Clear Fountain" |
| Andante | Moderately slow tempo |
| Annexe | Appendix/Annex |
| "Au Clair de la Lune" | "By the Light of the Moon" |
| "Berceuse de la Pluie" | "Lullaby of the Rain" |
| Bonne volonté | Good will |
| Cadeau | Gift |
| Café | Café / Coffee |
| Chanson | Song |
| Clair | Clear |
| Communale | Public |
| Conservatoire | Music conservatory |
| Curiosités et Fils de Rien | Curiosities and Sons of Nothing |
| Dernier | Last |
| Dimanche | Sunday |
| Écoute | Listen |
| École | School |
| Enfant(s) | Child(ren) |
| Étude | Study |
| Fin | End / Finish |
| Fleur | Flower |
| Forgeron de la Pluie (Le) | Blacksmith of Rain |

| French | Pronunciation |
|---|---|
| "Frère Jacques" | "Brother John" (nursery rhyme) |
| Gardien (Le) | The Keeper |
| Hôtel de Ville | City Hall |
| Hospice des Enfants-Trouvés | Orphanage for found children |
| Jour de Saint-Julien (Le) | The Day of Saint Julien |
| Maison (La) | The House |
| Maître | Master / Teacher |
| Marché | Market |
| Merci | Thank you |
| Monsieur | Mr. |
| Musique | Music |
| Orphelin, sans demeure | Orphan, without a home |
| Ouvrage (L') | The Work / The Masterpiece |
| Parapluie | Umbrella |
| Pluie | Rain |
| Rousse | Policeman |

Thank you for spending your time on this book. If anything in these pages stayed with you—a line, a scene, a thought—I'd love to hear about it.

If you're willing, please leave an honest review. It's one of the simplest ways to support an author and help the right readers discover the story.

Scan the QR code to reach my review hub and choose your preferred site (Amazon, Goodreads, etc.).

Thank you—truly.

wb Arnaud

www.ingramcontent.com/pod-product-compliance
Lightning Source LLC
Chambersburg PA
CBHW060406310726